PRAISE FOR
ZOMBIE P.I.

"Sharp and funny; this zombie detective rocks!"

—Patricia Briggs

"A dead detective, a wimpy vampire, and other interesting characters from the supernatural side of the street make Death Warmed Over *an unpredictable walk on the weird side. Prepare to be entertained."*

—Charlaine Harris

"Master storyteller Kevin J. Anderson's Death Warmed Over *is wickedly funny, deviously twisted and enormously satisfying. This is a big juicy bite of zombie goodness. Two decaying thumbs up!"*

—Jonathan Maberry

"A darkly funny, wonderfully original detective tale."

—Kelley Armstrong

"The Dan Shamble books are great fun."

—Simon R. Green

"A good detective doesn't let a little thing like getting murdered slow him down, and I got a kick out of Shamble trying to solve a

series of oddball cases, including his own. He's the kind of zombie you want to root for, and his cases are good, light hearted fun."

—Larry Correia, *New York Times* bestselling author of the Monster Hunter International series

"Anderson's world-building skills shine through in his latest series, Dan Shamble, P.I. Readers looking for a mix of humor, romance, and good old-fashioned detective work will be delighted by this offering."

—*RT Book Reviews* (4 stars)

"Kevin J. Anderson's Death Warmed Over *and his Dan Shamble, Zombie P.I. novels are truly pure reading enjoyment—funny, intriguing—and written in a voice that charms the reader from the first page and onward. Smart, savvy—fresh, incredibly clever! I love these books."

—Heather Graham, *New York Times* bestselling author of the Krewe of Hunters series

DOUBLE-BOOKED

A DAN SHAMBLE, ZOMBIE P.I. ADVENTURE

KEVIN J. ANDERSON

WFP

WORDFIRE PRESS

EBook ISBN: 978-1-68057-351-0
Trade Paperback ISBN: 978-1-68057-350-3 Dust Jacket Hardcover ISBN: 978-1-68057-352-7
Library of Congress Control Number: 2022936377
Cover design by miblart
Kevin J. Anderson, Art Director
Published by
WordFire Press, LLC
PO Box 1840
Monument CO 80132
Kevin J. Anderson & Rebecca Moesta, Publishers
WordFire Press eBook Edition 2022
WordFire Press Trade Paperback Edition 2022
WordFire Press Hardcover Edition 2022
Printed in the USA
Join our WordFire Press Readers Group for
sneak previews, updates, new projects, and giveaways.
Sign up at wordfirepress.com

DEADICATION

To my three grandsons

Harrison
Xavier
Teddy

Who always keep me at the top of my game with stupid
Grandpa jokes.

CHAPTER 1

I t's a black-tie gala, Beaux—fancy-schmancy," said Sheyenne, my beautiful ghost girlfriend. She hovered in front of me and fussed over my appearance like an obsessive-compulsive undertaker. "You can't wear this old sport jacket with bullet holes all over the front."

With zombie-stiff fingers I brushed at the lumpy black threads where the holes had been clumsily stitched up. "It's what I always wear."

"Not for special occasions." Sheyenne was gorgeous in a phantasmagorical evening gown with sapphire sequins, manifested to perfectly fit her curves.

"I don't have a black tie either," I pointed out. "A tie feels like a noose around my neck."

"You've never had a noose around your neck, so how would you know?" She drifted around me, checking my appearance. "And we need to do something about the bullet hole in your forehead. I have embalming putty in my desk drawer. Let's make tonight special."

We were in the offices of Chambeaux & Deyer Investigations, getting ready for the swanky reception at Howard Phillips Publishing. The event was a duty dance for our clients, but as a zombie I've done very little dancing. It doesn't turn out well when I try.

With a poltergeist nudge, Sheyenne opened the side drawer

of the receptionist's desk and pulled out a jar of mortician's putty. She let it hover in front of me until I took it from her insubstantial grip.

"For you, Spooky, I will even do without the hole in my head."

She gave me a seductive smile that would have made my heart melt, if my heart still functioned, and then added in an enticing tone. "There'll be hors d'oeuvres."

"Maybe little cocktail hotdogs!" said a dangerously cheerful voice. "With blood ketchup, my favorite."

Alvina, a spunky ten-year-old vampire girl, bounded across the office. She bubbled with more joyful energy than I'd ever possessed, even when I was alive. "I like playing dress up. This doesn't suck at all." My half-daughter wore a teal blouse with sparkly crystals on the front and a loose chiffon skirt over a silky underskirt. Her blonde hair was in pigtails, and her hopeful grin displayed pointed white fangs.

I knew I had to make the best of the situation. "I still have the dark suit I was buried in. I could wear that—it's been dry-cleaned, all the dirt stains removed."

A few years ago, after a case went sour and I got shot in a dark alley, I was buried in the Green Lawn Cemetery. But thanks to the magic released in the Big Uneasy, I clawed my way up through six feet of dirt and went right back to work. Back from the dead and back on the case, and since then, Chambeaux & Deyer has had a string of satisfied clients.

"You can look pretty snappy when you want to, Beaux." Sheyenne glowed. "You always keep yourself well-preserved."

"Yay!" Alvina ran to the closet in my office and pulled out the dark suit hanging there, still wrapped in its plastic dry-cleaning bag.

The little vampire girl had only recently come to stay with

us in the Unnatural Quarter, abandoned by her sour-tempered mother Rhonda, who couldn't deal with the fact that her child now had fangs. I harbored doubts that Rhonda herself was human, but that's a different matter. We had history....

We call Alvina my "half-daughter" because we aren't entirely sure whether I'm her father or if it's my best human friend, Officer Toby McGoohan. We both hooked up with Rhonda at about the same time—call it simultaneous temporary insanity, from which we fortunately both recovered.

The poor kid became a vampire through an inept blood transfusion after a skateboarding accident. Because vampire blood made permanent changes to DNA, paternity tests were no longer valid, so McGoo and I could never know the real answer. Alvina was a bright and cheery presence, and we all took care of her. Alvina would come with us to the book-launch gala, since McGoo was working tonight.

I shrugged out of my usual bullet-riddled sport jacket and donned the formal suit, while poltergeist Sheyenne whipped and swirled the tie around my neck, expertly tying a neat Oxford knot, a skill I had never mastered. "I don't know what I'd do without you."

Meanwhile, Alvina had fun plugging putty into the hole in my forehead, giggling as she probed with her forefinger.

Although it was a formal event, I drew the line at giving up my fedora. Even if the color clashed with my funeral suit, it's my trademark. I'm a zombie P.I.

Robin Deyer, my human lawyer partner, emerged from her office dressed in a sapphire silk blazer and skirt. Her black hair was clipped back, her features highlighted by dainty gold earrings and subtle plum lipstick.

I gave a slight bow. "You look stunning."

Robin straightened, exuding more confidence than I could

manage on my best day. "My aim is less to stun people, Dan, than to impress them. I want to be seen as the best damn lawyer in the Quarter." She adjusted the thin gold chain around her neck. "This launch party is important for our clients, and it could generate new business."

The two witches Mavis and Alma Wannovich work on the editorial staff of the largest publisher in the Quarter. In exchange for letting them base a book series on my real cases, Mavis and Alma perform a monthly maintenance spell on me to counteract the wear and tear an unnatural detective is bound to encounter during the normal course of business.

Tonight, Howard Phillips Publishing would announce a big upcoming release, hoping to drum up media attention and also, presumably, to get rid of surplus cocktail weenies and blood ketchup.

Admiring my three lovely companions, I insisted on serving as chauffeur. We left the front door and stepped out onto the street, feeling like a million bucks … in sharp contrast to our rusty and battered vehicle, a lime-green Ford Maverick that we had affectionately dubbed the "Pro Bono Mobile."

We climbed in, and I settled behind the steering wheel, while Robin made sure Alvina was buckled in the back seat.

"We should have rented a limo," Alvina commented.

Shimmering in the passenger seat, Sheyenne said, "Style is in your heart and mind, honey."

The hinge creaked as I pulled the door shut. The engine coughed, hiccupped, sneezed, and snorted like an orc with a severe head cold, but finally caught. "Don't worry, I can park out of sight."

I shifted into gear and lurched along the bright nighttime boulevard.

CHAPTER 2

The publishing headquarters rose above the other buildings in the surrounding blocks, since Howard Phillips Publishing aspired to high literature. They catered to monster readers, ghostly historians, powerful wizards, necromancers, and amateur magicians.

A dried-up fountain was the centerpiece of a pedestrian plaza in front of the main entrance. The ground-level lobby held a company bookstore, and right now workers were setting up for a public book signing to be held after the gala VIP reception.

Alvina flashed our invitations to get us past the lobby guard, a burly uniformed golem named Grundy (according to the name imprinted on his clay forehead). We went to the main elevator bank and rode up to the publishing offices on the thirteenth floor.

I emerged with Sheyenne on one arm and Alvina on the other, proud to be their escort. Robin walked ahead, leading the way.

The reception was already in full swing. Several dozen guests milled about, dressed to the nines (or even higher numbers). A band played quiet, boring jazz. A mummy whisked brushes over a set of drums, a skeleton tinkled the keys of a piano, and a bald mad scientist in a lab coat plucked the strings of a bass.

At a portable bar, an alchemist mixologist poured chemicals from beakers to create smoking red libations, which he dispensed into fluted glasses. Igors in tuxedoes carried silver platters of drinks and drifted among the guests.

"Look, little hot dogs!" Alvina bounded over to a hunched Igor who balanced a tray in each hand. The miniature weenies were skewered with toothpicks whose ends had been carefully blunted, so as not to intimidate vampire guests.

Robin went to order a sparkling water, and I snagged a glass of something green for the sake of appearances. I would have preferred a beer at the Goblin Tavern, but this was a high-class event.

Alvina came running back with an hors d'oeuvre plate filled with cocktail weenies smothered in steaming crimson liquid.

At the back of the room, I noticed two human guests hovering near the wall, a man and a woman who looked just as odd as the unnaturals. The woman wore old-fashioned lavender skirts, a corset, and a bustle that made her butt pop up in an archaically attractive way. Her brown hair was done up in curls under a frilly bonnet, and the heavy rouge on her cheeks made her look like a granny apple doll.

Her male companion wore a Dickensian frock coat, cravat, and a pocket watch on a chain tucked into a paisley satin vest. He accentuated the look with bushy muttonchop sideburns. These two sure must like uncomfortable clothes a lot more than I did. In addition to the odd costume, the man had a leather bag over his shoulder that held a rolled tube, like some ancient chart.

"I wonder if they're from a retro-historical society," Sheyenne said.

Robin considered. "Maybe it's publicity for a new Howard Phillips classics line."

A large sow waddled up to us, accompanied by a frumpy, heavyset woman in a black dress and tall pointy hat. "Mr. Shamble, I'm so glad you came!" She had a long, hooked nose to which she added a wart for special occasions, and wiry black hair modeled after a steel-wool pad.

"Good evening, Mavis." I bent down to pat the head of her sow sister, who snuffled and nudged my pant leg. "And you, too, Alma."

Sheyenne drifted beside me. "We're very happy to show our support."

Robin also joined us, sipping her sparkling water. "Congratulations. You two have worked very hard to get this book ready for publication."

Mavis cackled. "Indeed. No spelling errors this time!"

The sow grunted an enthusiastic affirmation. It was a painful reminder of the love spell that had gone horribly wrong, due to unfortunate typos, which permanently transformed Alma Wannovich into her porcine form.

Alvina scratched behind the pig's floppy ears, much to the transformed witch's delight.

"Tonight you'll meet our boss," Mavis said, and when Alma snorted a correction, her sister nodded. "*Bosses*, plural! Sorry— both Howard and Philip Phillips. Come join us—they're about to make the big announcement."

We worked our way through the crowd to the cleared speaking area. On the way, Alvina snagged a few more cocktail weenies.

Standing on watch at the edge of the speaking area, a blue-uniformed beat cop hooked his thumbs through his belt loops, surveying the crowd. He saw me and cocked an eyebrow. "Hey, Shamble!"

"I didn't know you were going to be here, McGoo. You said you were on duty."

A flush came to his freckled face. "I said I had to work—hired as extra security, guarding whatever needs to be guarded. I get paid overtime to stand around and look intimidating."

"You're doing the first half of the job pretty well," I teased.

Alvina ran over and wrapped her arms around his waist. "Half-Daddy!"

"Hey, Al."

The band reached an easy-listening crescendo, and the mummy drummer struck the cymbals like a ceremonial gong at a pyramid temple. The crowd noise dwindled.

Mavis leaned close to me. "This is so exciting!"

Two men emerged from the barricaded executive publishing offices in the rear. I had never seen both of the Phillips brothers together. They were exactly the same height, with matching gray tweed jackets, trim beards, long faces, and paternal expressions. One man wore a black top hat while the other sported a black bowler.

The identical twins walked in unison into the cleared area. "Thank you for coming to this momentous occasion," said the man in the top hat. "I am Howard Phillips, and this is my brother Philip Phillips."

The man in the bowler nodded. "We're the publishers." His smile cracked into a wider grin. "You probably figured that out."

To my left, Alma let out a muffled squeal.

"Tonight, we announce the greatest book release in the history of our publishing company," Howard said. "A special facsimile of the original *Necronomicon*." He paused for a round of cheers and gasps. "Our commemorative twelfth anniversary edition of the classic tome."

Philip ran a finger along the edge of his bowler hat. "Twelfth *plus one*, due to unavoidable production delays."

Howard cut in. "This powerful, magical tome truly changed the entire world, by causing the Big Uneasy and bringing all of the unnaturals back twelve years ago."

"Thirteen," Philip interrupted, "due to unavoidable production delays."

Grumbling, Howard adjusted his top hat. "Yes, technically thirteen years, but the catalog copy remains the same."

As the Phillips brothers struggled to upstage each other, I could see why they didn't often appear together in public.

Philip said, "At this preorder launch party, we are proud to reveal the cover and tell you about the different states of the book editions."

Howard waved a flyer in his left hand. "No other edition of the *Necronomicon* is finer, a book worthy of such a momentous date, the twelfth anniversary."

"Thirteenth," Philip muttered.

"We have a silver edition bound in calfskin, a gold edition bound in goatskin." Howard drew a deep breath to build the suspense.

But Philip blurted out the rest of the announcement. "And a platinum limited edition bound in human skin. Makes a perfect gift."

The audience members spoke in awed whispers, many asking about the pricing structure.

Alvina came over and tugged on my sleeve. "Can I have a copy of the book? I like to read."

"We'll see," I said.

Handing me her plate, she rushed back to McGoo to tug on his blue uniform sleeve. "Can I have a copy? I like to read."

I was happy to see her so excited.

Mavis nudged me with her elbow. "Just you wait, Mr. Shamble. This evening gets better and better."

I plucked the last tiny hotdog from Alvina's plate. "Better than this?"

Howard signaled the mummy drummer, who rattled out a loud drumroll. "To ensure the complete accuracy of our facsimile edition, we have obtained the original, actual, genuine, guaranteed *first* copy of the *Necronomicon* to display right here in our publishing offices."

Philip broke in, "It will provide inspiration and dread for our employees. And serve as a convenient reference for production."

The executive office doors opened again, and a group of elves brought out an ornate pedestal, on which rested a massive book enclosed in a transparent case. The knee-high elves rolled the pedestal forward on squeaking wheels. Dressed in green forest garb, the creatures danced and pranced, and when the display stand reached the middle of the floor, they used awls, hammers, bolts, and wrenches to anchor it in place.

"Complete security," said Philip. "This original book is on special loan from the Unnatural Quarter Metropolitan Museum."

The ancient book lay open, its yellowed pages covered with handwritten letters in dark red ink, purported to be blood. The edges were ragged as if well worn. A couple of the corners were folded over, probably where some ancient necromancer had marked his place while reading.

The front cover was propped up to display its scaly leather and etched runes. The title *NECRONOMICON* stood out in ornate letters, along with the embossed tag *National Bestseller!*

I had seen the original volume in a special gallery in the museum. In fact, I'd helped rescue it from a disastrous outflux of sewage perpetrated by an underground slumlord. Now, though, the tome was high and dry on the thirteenth floor of Howard Phillips Publishing.

I nodded to Mavis. "Now I'm impressed. I didn't think the museum would let it out of their sight."

"Oh, but that's not all," the witch said. "Wait for it!" Her sow sister wiggled, snorted, and squealed. I was reminded of teenage girls waiting for the arrival of the current transient pop singer.

Howard said, "And now, to mark the occasion, we have a special celebrity guest, who will sign autographs and take special photos *with you!*"

Philip interjected, "For a fee."

Howard raised his voice like an all-star wrestling announcer. "We now present to you, the woman who started it all! Back when the planets aligned and the moon was in the proper phase … the fifty-year-old virgin librarian who spilled her blood on the *Necronomicon* and caused the Big Uneasy itself!"

Philip shouted, "Miss! Stella! Artois!" He and his brother flailed their hands, cheering like Kermit the frog.

Robin's large, brown eyes widened. "Now, this is unexpected."

"I thought she never appeared in public," Sheyenne said.

The elves flung the executive office doors wide and stepped back. The lounge band played their version of a dramatic fanfare.

Nervous and uncomfortable, overwhelmed by the weight of fame and celebrity, a mousy woman in her sixties ventured forward. She peered around through wire-rimmed glasses.

Stella Artois, the librarian who changed the world.

CHAPTER 3

As the meek librarian ventured into the sudden roar of applause, I could see she didn't like the attention one bit. Her face turned beet red as she saw the giddy fans with their wide eyes and bright smiles (some with pointy or jagged teeth). The pesky elves nudged her forward, encouraging her toward the speaking area.

Sheyenne's ectoplasmic form glowed brighter. Alvina bounced up and down, clapping her hands, and even Robin seemed gobsmacked (and I'd never had occasion to use "gobsmacked" in a sentence before). Robin whispered, "The whole world was changed by that woman's act."

"Accident is a better word for it," I said.

Thirteen years ago, while working in the rare-books section of the main branch, this fifty-year-old quiet librarian had cut her finger and spilled a drop of blood on the cursed pages of the *Necronomicon*. Unluckily for her, but luckily for unnaturals everywhere, that fateful papercut occurred at midnight under a full moon and an astrologically rare alignment of planets. A real red-letter night for stargazers—and high sorcery.

Now, Stella was in way over her head, and she looked very uncomfortable to be the center of attention. Before she could flee back into the executive offices, Howard and Philip beckoned her toward the *Necronomicon* podium. "Come here, dear," Philip said in a warm voice. "These people are your fans."

Howard's smile was even brighter than his brother's. "They're here to celebrate you ... as well as our new edition."

Prodded by the elves, Stella moved reluctantly, looking like a rabbit being hunted by a pterodactyl. She was obviously uncomfortable (perhaps confused about why a pterodactyl would appear in that simile).

A female werewolf in a white cocktail dress howled, "Thank you, Stella!"

A mummy yelled so loudly that dust puffed through his mouth bandages. "We love you, Stella!"

"Stella! Stella!" the crowd chanted, and the bass player and drummer picked up the beat, prodding the audience until everyone was shouting, "Stella! Stella! Stella! Stella!" The mummy drummer crashed the cymbal again.

As security, McGoo stood square-shouldered, trying to look reassuring. His hands were within easy reach of his police special revolver on one hip and the police extra-special silver-bullet revolver in the opposite holster.

Howard raised his hands for silence as the tentative librarian approached the podium. Philip shook the timid woman's hand.

Stella Artois had permed, dyed-brown hair that required little maintenance. Her sensible gray dress was obviously a Sunday-best outfit, far outshadowed by the evening gowns present at the gala. In an attempt to spruce her up, someone had pinned a large lily corsage on her shoulder.

Before the chant could break out again, Howard announced, "Stella will be personally autographing a thousand signature sheets for our special platinum edition of the *Necronomicon*. In honor of her incredible service, not only to the

Unnatural Quarter but to monsters all around the world, my brother and I have reserved Lettered Copy A exclusively for her."

Philip jumped in. "But Lettered Copy B, and all the other letters—"

"—and numbers," Howard said.

"—are available for preorder to our special fans and supporters tonight."

"Paperback edition to follow," Howard added, though he kept his voice low to discourage orders of the lower-priced option.

Blushing, Stella stared at the *Necronomicon* on display, as if the book might attack her.

Philip prodded her. "Say a few words. Everybody looks up to you."

The librarian shuffled her feet—sensible shoes, I saw—and cleared her throat. At first, her voice came out as *"Meep!"* but then she found her words. "Ahem, thank you for coming. My ... I'm embarrassed, but honored. Twelve years ago, I accidentally did something that would change my life forever."

Philip whispered loudly, *"Thirteen* years ago."

She blinked behind her wire-rimmed glasses, her train of thought derailed. "I know, Mr. Phillips, but I wrote this speech last year, when the book was supposed to be released."

The publisher backed away, mumbling about unavoidable production delays.

Stella found her words again. "Because librarians handle books and turn pages all day, papercuts are an occupational hazard. I didn't look at the astrological calendar, I paid no attention to the phases of the moon, or I never would have—"

"We love you, Stella!" the werewolf woman howled again.

"You're our hero!" a zombie rasped.

His zombie date nudged him hard in the ribs, which made a squelching sound. *"Heroine."*

"My, at the time, I didn't know that real magic existed," Stella continued. "And now it's everywhere. The world is full of it." She had that hunted look again as she flicked her glance around the crowd. "Now *you're* everywhere!"

Sheyenne flickered beside me, showing her concern. "I hope they didn't coerce that poor woman into making this appearance against her wishes."

Robin shook her head. "She likely signed a publicity clause in her contract. If Ms. Artois was paid an endorsement fee for this new edition, she would have been required to participate in certain promotional activities."

Again, I noted the couple standing against the wall in their old-fashioned costumes. Unlike the smiling and cheering unnaturals, the pair looked serious, even grim.

Several invited reporters took notes on pads, while others held up digital recorders to capture Stella's every word. I recognized one vampire columnist known for her biting commentary—CJ Ananaya, who used the friendly letters "CJ" to lull her victims into a false sense of security so they would make embarrassing comments, while "Ananaya" was a name you could really sink your teeth into.

As the celebrity librarian searched for words, Ananaya called out a question. "Tell us about this virgin sacrifice, Ms. Artois! How, ahhh, bloody was it?"

Stella's forehead wrinkled with concern. "It was just a papercut. Only a tiny drop of blood."

"A drop is all the magic required!" crowed a necromancer in the audience, raising a champagne glass.

"It did sting, though," Stella admitted.

"The pain must have amplified the magic!" said a gray-robed wizard, with a knowing nod to the necromancer. "Not to mention the sacrifice she made in staying a virgin for fifty years."

The vampire columnist interrupted again. "Now, one more question about the virgin sacrifice ..." She emphasized the word *virgin*. "How did you prepare for that moment? What challenges did you overcome to keep yourself pure all your life so you could restore magic and bring unnaturals back to the world?"

Stella flushed even deeper red. "Are you implying that I stayed a virgin *on purpose*? All my life? I was just shy! I didn't know how to talk to boys, and I didn't date much." She sniffed.

The crowd murmured, and other reporters got ready to call out their questions, but CJ Ananaya dominated them all. "A final question, Ms. Artois—are you *still* a virgin?"

The librarian gasped, and Robin spun toward the reporter. "That's quite enough!"

Sheyenne brightened in rage. "I'll punch her fangs in!"

"What's a virgin?" Alvina asked.

Mortally embarrassed, Stella adjusted the collar of her dress. "Well, if you must know, I got quite a bit of attention after the Big Uneasy happened. People constantly calling, wanting to meet with me, take me out to dinner." She giggled, lost in thought. "Oh, the suggestive letters and photographs I received! I didn't know people could take selfies like that." Finding her resolve again, she glared at the vampire columnist. "But it's none of your business!"

The audience murmured, and some chuckled.

A male werewolf gave a loud wolf whistle. "She isn't!"

The man in the old-fashioned costume tucked away his gold pocket watch and shouted out, "Does that mean you can't fix it, then?"

"Fix it?" Stella asked.

In full security-guard mode, McGoo tensed up, expecting trouble. I stood ready to help if things got out of hand.

The old-fashioned woman straightened her lacy bonnet. "You can't undo the Big Uneasy if you're not still a virgin."

"I ... I never—" Stella stammered.

With a dramatic gesture, the old-fashioned man pulled a rolled-up paper tube from his satchel and extended it to his prim companion. "Help me with this please, Violet." Together, they unrolled a long banner with ornate Victorian letters that proclaimed *Remember G-O-D!*

"Remember!" the man shouted.

"Remember!" the woman echoed.

Instead of a rousing response, the rest of the crowd just looked at them, perplexed.

"Now, now, this is not a religious gathering," Howard said, trying to regain control of the event.

"Religious gathering?" Puzzled by the response, the old-fashioned man peered down at his banner.

The woman also squinted at the words. "What does he mean, Rupert?"

The old-fashioned man slowly realized the cause for confusion. "Ah, I see! No, no, it's an acronym. Remember G-O-D."

He paused, and his companion filled in, "The *Good Old Days*. Remember the Good Old Days! Back before the Big Uneasy."

Together, they raised the banner higher. "We're the Olde Tymers, a group of concerned citizens trying to restore the world to how it was before all these ... monsters arrived uninvited."

Burly and intimidating, McGoo strode up to the Olde Tymers. "This is a private event. A celebration. I have to ask you to leave." He confiscated the banner and gave the costumed party crashers the bum's rush toward the elevator. Many of the grumbling unnaturals present—including myself —would have been happy to help chase them out.

Next to the *Necronomicon* stand, Philip raised his hands for calm. "Terribly sorry about that unfortunate interruption."

Mavis Wannovich adjusted her pointy hat, looking down her hooked nose. "Some people just can't accept change."

The large sow snorted in agreement.

After an awkward moment, the band started playing again. The mad-scientist bass player plucked his strings, and the mummy artfully used his brushes to make the drums sound like someone sweeping a floor. In atonal contrast to his bandmates, the skeleton whipped up a bright ragtime melody on the piano.

Howard placed a reassuring hand on Stella's shoulder. "Everyone, please finish your drinks and move downstairs to the lobby bookstore. Ms. Artois will be happy to sign leaflets, photos, and any old copies of the *Necronomicon* you have in your collection."

"For a modest signing fee," Philip added.

Mavis raised her hand and pointed to me. "Excuse me! We also have special guests Dan Chambeaux and his partner Robin Deyer, the inspiration for our wildly popular Shamble & Die series. They'll autograph their books as well."

I glanced uncomfortably at Robin, but Alvina beamed. Seeing how happy and proud the little vampire girl was made me resolved to face even a zombie horde of fans. "And you can be our assistant."

CHAPTER 4

The skyscraper's ground-floor lobby held a bookstore featuring titles published by Howard Phillips. An adjacent café served coffee, blood drinks, and cookies.

After chasing the two Olde Tymers out of the building, McGoo paced outside the street entrance. He and Grundy, the lobby golem guard, tried to organize the customers who had started to gather for that night's public event. "Not yet! Still finishing setup."

One of the troll hostesses erected a sandwich board outside the door. "Signing Tonight! STELLA ARTOIS!!! Virgin librarian responsible for Big Uneasy!!!" In chalk, someone had inserted the handwritten word "former" before "virgin" and also before "librarian."

Inside, the trolls had draped streamers of black crepe paper along the bookshelves. Bats fluttered around like party favors, and contract-employee spiders enhanced the interior decorating with intricate webs.

The Igors came down from the gala, still dressed in tuxedos. They slid tables into place and stacked copies of the old trade edition of the *Necronomicon*, which Stella would sign. The chair behind the main signing table was a carved wooden throne, possibly purchased at a moving sale from Dracula's castle. An ornate pewter goblet of water sat next to a neat line of signing pens for the guest of honor.

Next, the Igors pulled a wobbly card table from a side room and set up two folding chairs, while one of the troll hostesses made handwritten paper tents labeled SHAMBLE and DIE. She gave us an apologetic look. "Sorry, we weren't sure you would be here."

I glanced at Alvina. "We can't stay long. She needs to get to bed."

"Not until sunup," the girl insisted. "It's not a school night."

Since the Igors were busy preparing for Stella Artois, we helped out by going into the bookstore section to retrieve our books from the shelves.

I hadn't realized what I was getting into when Mavis Wannovich proposed a line of fictionalized adventures based on my detective work. The publisher had hired a ghostwriter —a vampire woman named Linda Bullwer—who published the books under a pen name because she liked her privacy.

Five novels in the Shamble & Die series had come out, and the critics hailed them as "silly, lowbrow entertainment at best." The covers were garish but eye-catching, and the titles sounded corny. Nevertheless, the series had certainly drummed up business for us, and Robin and I were happy to sign copies for our readers. I think Alvina was more impressed than anybody.

I carried a stack of *Slimy Underbelly* paperbacks, while Alvina found ten copies of *Tastes Like Chicken*, the first novel that had featured her character on the cover. Robin retrieved both of the story collections. I stacked the books on our wobbly signing table, while Sheyenne arranged them more artfully. The Igors found another folding chair so Alvina could sit between us, and she took her position as assistant very seriously.

When it was almost time to let the crowds in, Grundy stood

next to Stella's elaborate throne, while McGoo stationed himself by our table. He got that look in his eye that told me he was going to offer an unsolicited joke, and I braced myself. "Hey Shamble, you know what a vegetarian zombie eats?" He paused only a beat before answering, *"Graaaiiins!"*

Alvina giggled.

"No fair—that's a repeat," I said. "And the joke wasn't any better the first time."

"Okay, since you want another one." He gave a cockeyed grin. "What does a *Scottish* zombie eat?"

That was new. "What?"

McGoo's smile widened. *"Bairns!"*

Alvina giggled even harder at that one.

I pinched the bridge of my nose as if I had a headache.

"You want more?" McGoo asked. "I got a million of 'em."

Fortunately, Grundy flung open the doors, and customers entered the store, all of them looking for the famous librarian, who hadn't yet arrived from upstairs. Ghosts and ghouls, werewolves (full-furred ones as well as monthly transformers), a pair of lizard demons on a date, a mummy with a rolled-up papyrus (which he wanted autographed), even booksellers carrying boxes of stock from their own inventory.

Sheyenne hovered close behind us, looking at the empty throne chair behind all the *Necronomicons*. "I can't remember the last time Stella Artois made a public appearance. This is a big deal."

"She has drawn quite a crowd," Robin said.

The Igors herded the customers into a neat line, and the troll hostesses took care of the cash register. The lanes had been roped off, routing the customers past the café where they could be enticed to purchase refreshments while they waited. Another Igor squatted on a high barstool next to Stella's throne with a cash box so he could accept money for the autographs and selfies.

A freight elevator opened in the back, and the publishing twins strolled out like emcees to a game show, warming up the crowd. "And here she is ... Ms. Stella Artois, the librarian of the evening!"

Another burly clay golem walked behind the nervous librarian as an implacable bodyguard. The name written on his gray forehead was also Grundy. The publisher must have gotten a quantity discount from the rent-a-golem service.

Stella looked overwhelmed and out of place as a covey of elves nudged her toward the ornate signing chair. With help from Grundy Two, she climbed into the awkward throne and sighed in preemptive exhaustion upon seeing the stack of *Necronomicons* and the line of fans. One elf handed her a pen, while another adjusted the water goblet to be in convenient reach.

A group of school-age goblins clutched used paperbacks of the *Necronomicon*, School Edition. They chittered, poking one another, as if they hadn't had their ADHD medicine, while their teacher stood behind them blank-faced, no longer even noticing the rambunctiousness.

Impatient customers began nudging and jostling for autographs. Some held up their phones to take surreptitious photos until the first Grundy strolled over. "You want a picture, fill out a card and pay the fee."

Alvina hopped off her chair, full of energy. "Speaking of social media," she said, although no one had mentioned social media. She pulled out her iPhone and began taking photos of the customers, videos of the excited crowd.

When the second Grundy glowered, Robin explained, "We're also guest authors, and Miss Alvina is our publicist."

The busy kid took pictures of Stella Artois unhappily auto-graphing books while her assigned Igor accepted cash for the signing box. She also took photos of me in my funeral suit, zooming in on the fedora and my bullet hole, then a shot of me and Robin, me and Sheyenne. Alvina took a selfie with the three of us, and ran around the table to take a picture with her other half-daddy. When the enthusiastic girl started to get in the way, though, Sheyenne took her off to the café to get a sugar cookie.

In line, the people pestered poor Stella with countless fan questions, asking the meanings of obscure passages in the *Necronomicon*, "helpfully" pointing out passages they disliked, or egregious typographical errors. (Mavis and Alma Wannovich took offense, reassuring them that the new 12 + 1 special anniversary edition had been completely reproofed.)

In exasperation, Stella said, "You know I didn't write the *Necronomicon*? No, I don't recall that passage. No, I wasn't in charge of the typesetting." She grew even more frazzled when fans asked her opinions on *The Lord of the Rings* or the latest *Star Wars* movie.

Robin and I sat behind our own stack of books at the table, unnoticed in the hubbub, until a frog demon stopped by our table and made a sound like a belch deep in his throat. "Awww, I didn't know you were going to be here! Awww, I would have brought my books."

"You could always buy a new copy," Robin suggested, lifting a copy from the stack. "Dan and I would both sign it."

The frog demon flicked a forked tongue over his nose slits. "No thanks."

A frumpy vampire woman in cat's-eye glasses and a beehive hairdo slipped up behind us and leaned close to my ear. "The

Shamble & Die novels sell much better online. People like to binge read the whole series."

I recognized our vampire ghostwriter. "Good evening, Ms. Bullwer."

"In this place, I'm known as Penny Dreadful, since that's the name on the book covers."

I offered her my chair. "You should be the one autographing. You're the real author."

"But you're the inspiration," said Linda Bullwer.

"Are you working on a new novel in the series?" Robin asked. "It's been a while since the last book came out, and that was only a story collection."

"I've been busy with other writing assignments—a large new project for Howard Phillips Publishing, which I hope I can announce soon. But the next Shamble & Die is always on my mind." She ran a finger over the new cover art for *Tastes Like Chicken* and glanced at Alvina coming back from the café, nibbling on a sugar cookie. "That's quite a good cover, great depiction." She clucked her tongue. "Too much sugar for that little girl, though. She'll get cavities in those fangs."

"She brushes every morning before she goes to sleep," I said.

Outside, a commotion occurred in the pedestrian plaza. More Olde Tymers protesters had arrived to share their nostalgic view of the good old days. The old-fashioned woman in the lavender dress and the man with muttonchop sideburns were joined by what looked like extras from a Jane Austen movie adaptation. They made a surly, if stylish, crowd.

Working together, the group unrolled a long banner that said *Remember G-O-D*. One dapper man with a handlebar mustache waved a sign. "We miss the good old days." The Olde

Tymers began to sing, not protest songs, but a round of "Auld Lang Syne."

McGoo growled deep in his throat, and the bookstore customers looked uneasily at the protest outside. Grundy and Grundy lumbered toward the door.

By now, the crowd had dwindled inside the store, and Howard capped the line. "Thank you all for coming."

Philip went down the line, prepping books and hurrying the customers along. Stella Artois scrawled her signature in each of the remaining copies, impatient to leave.

Howard said, "We hired you for security, Officer McGoohan. Would you please escort Ms. Artois home?"

McGoo looked at the two Grundy golems. "Why not one of the clay guys?"

Philip said, "The fine print in their reanimation scrolls prevents them from leaving the building."

Stella looked at McGoo, full of hope, and he tipped his cap toward her. "I'll get you there safe and sound, ma'am, a real police escort." He gestured her toward the back exit, then gave Alvina a playful chuck under the chin. "See you later, Al. You, too, Shamble."

The librarian scuttled after him as the rest of the crowd dispersed.

CHAPTER 5

The next day we were right back at work, waiting for cases. Alvina calls them adventures.

Chambeaux & Deyer Investigations is in a "landmark, charming, and conveniently located" commercial building—in other words, a run-down, two-story wreck in the seedy part of town. The landlord took a few liberties when describing the place in a new brochure. Office space was always available since tenants kept moving out when businesses went bankrupt, perpetrators fled, or proprietors moved on to brighter horizons. In the past month alone, several new tenants had moved in, and we hadn't had a chance to meet them yet.

Robin and I had set up shop here not long after the Big Uneasy. A lawyer and a private investigator seemed like a natural partnership, even as the world around us turned decidedly unnatural. Now, the fact that I'm undead helps with our advertising, though I would have preferred to remain alive, all things considered.

After a brief morning errand to serve eviction papers on a blood-beast infestation, I headed back to the offices. I entered the building and climbed stiffly up the creaking stairs—or maybe it was just my joints creaking. At the upper landing, I encountered our stoop-shouldered building superintendent, a ghoul named Renfeld.

Renfeld had leprous skin and tangled hair, the matted curls held in place with thick styling product, or maybe greasy residue from lack of hygiene. His eyes leaked a milky fluid, as did his nose, and droplets ran down to his chin and plopped onto the discolored hallway carpet. Sometimes late at night I would hear the whir and hum of an industrial steam cleaner that he shoved down the hall.

The ghoul superintendent nudged an offending lump of hair out of his eyes and greeted me. "Morning, Shamble. Just going about my daily rounds."

His rounds were, in fact, straight lines, back and forth, back and forth. The ghoul would shuffle-walk down to the end of the hall, regard the fire exit sign, then turn around and shuffle back to the stairs that led down to the ground floor. He'd repeat the process until he considered his rounds completed. Often, while I worked in the quiet offices, I found his regular sliding footsteps down in the hall soothing, like a white-noise generator.

"Any good cases today?" he asked.

I adjusted my fedora. "The usual. And the cases don't solve themselves."

The ghoul inhaled a snort, which skirled a loop of mucous deep into his sinus passages. "You know, I read that new book of yours, Mr. Shamble. *Slimy Underbelly.*"

"It's not actually *my* book. The real author's name is on the cover, Penny Dreadful."

"I'm in that book," Renfeld said. I couldn't tell if he felt insulted or pleased.

"Just a character inspired by you," I said, uncomfortable with the implied fame. "And I don't really have any—"

"So, in that book, you forgot to mention how handsome I am! Even so, I include it in my Monster Match dating profile.

All the ghouls love to go out with a celebrity." He snurtled mucous up his other nostril. "Scores every time."

Before he could go further into his dating life, I slipped past him. "I better leave you to go about your rounds, Renfeld. I have a heavy caseload today."

Chin down and intent, the ghoul headed toward the end of the hall. Before he could turn around and come back to pick up the conversation again, I ducked into our offices.

Behind her reception desk, Sheyenne was organizing folders and studying records. She brightened when she saw me. "Morning, Beaux. Blood beasts all served?"

"They'll be evicted like an old scab soon enough," I said. I hung my fedora on the rack.

Alvina sat at a worktable adjacent to the front desk, staring at her phone and the open laptop. "I'm posting the pictures from last night on social media. Over two hundred Likes so far."

I slipped off my sport jacket. "I thought you particularly liked the cocktail weenies."

"Don't be silly! They like me and the pictures I take. It's all about branding and audience engagement."

Alvina had built up a large audience for her deeply personal blog, *I Was a Teenage Vampire*, where she talked about how her life had changed after receiving the tainted transfusion. Her worries about fitting in resonated with countless permanently preteen and teenage unnaturals. The kid is witty, clever, and articulate—traits that she certainly got from me.

She showed me her phone screen. "This one's already trending on Sick-Tok—when the Olde Tymers caused such a fuss."

"Are your followers very concerned about political movements?" I asked.

"Oh, I don't do politics at all. That's poison on social media." Alvina sounded stern. "Everybody's commenting on their costumes." She flicked through a parade of screen images. "Look, my Monstagram profile has a hundred new followers as of this morning."

She scrolled past photos of the gala event: Robin and me standing together, a closeup of Mavis and Alma Wannovich, the blur of Sheyenne, floating champagne glasses—either held by invisible men, or vampires who didn't show up in photographs.

Alvina tried to take selfies with important Chambeaux & Deyer clients, even if she didn't show up on her own feed, and neither did the vampire celebrities. The resulting pictures just showed empty walls or chairs, but she took care to write captions to explain what the photos were. Many images showed werewolves, mummies, or demons, all with outstretched arms draped over an empty space as tall as a ten-year-old girl.

"I added a link to the preorder form for Howard Phillips Publishing," Alvina said. "It'll sell lots of copies of the *Necronomicon*—I'm an influencer." She batted her eyelashes. "You're going to order me one, right? My birthday's coming up in the next year. I'll keep it on my bookshelf next to the Harry Potter books."

"The *Necronomicon* isn't really a kid's book."

"I'm not a kid."

"And it's expensive," Sheyenne pointed out.

Alvina was not to be deterred. "I can ask the publisher for a free copy in exchange for my influence." I think optimism is her superpower.

Robin came out of her office, masterfully changing the subject. "We got some new business from the gala last night. I'll be consulting on copyright matters for the Phillips brothers, with an eye toward infringement issues—bootleg editions, ebook pirates, and bit-torrent sites. It's like a game of Whack-a-Lizard. You take one pirate site down, and three more pop up."

Sheyenne drifted by to reshelve a copy of the copyright handbook on our main reference shelves. "But isn't the *Necronomicon* centuries old, written by a mad, possessed monk? Surely, it's in public domain by now."

"The authorship and provenance are in question," Robin said.

"Sounds complicated," Sheyenne said. "With a lot of billable hours."

I made a cup of really bad coffee and carried it to my office. Sheyenne had set out a stack of manila folders with cold cases and a separate stack of completed cases whose clients had not yet paid their bills. I knew which ones she wanted me to solve first. It looked like a day of dreary paperwork.

Fortunately, the office door burst open and the day's first desperate client came in.

CHAPTER 6

I could tell at a glance that this new client was going to be a handful. Literally.

She was about nineteen, pretty in a girl-next-door way, thin as a beanpole. She had waifish brown eyes, high cheekbones, a pointed chin. And four arms.

Not *forearms*, the part between your wrist and your elbow —although she had those too, of course. Four of them.

She used one hand to close the door behind her, while the other three hands flailed about in panic. She wore a gray wool sweater with two extra sleeves for her spare pair of arms cut from another sweater and sewn on by hand (with neat stitches, which suggested she had excellent dexterity).

"Please, you've got to help me!" she said. Even with the ragged edge of fear, her voice was sweet. Her eyes locked with mine.

I resisted saying, "We can lend you a hand," because she clearly didn't need another hand, and also because that would have sounded like a McGoo joke.

Alvina snapped pictures of the young woman, but Robin scolded her in a low voice, "You can't post those—client privacy issues."

I stepped up to welcome the young woman. "I'm Dan Chambeaux. Come in and tell us about your case." I extended a hand toward her, but I didn't know which one to shake.

Sheyenne had already withdrawn a blank new client form from the side drawer. "At Chambeaux & Deyer Investigations, we're always happy to help. Miss …?"

"My name is Mary." The girl shivered with terror, even though she was well-armed. "Mary Celeste, and it's gone! *Gone!* You've got to help me find it."

With one hand she brushed a tear from her cheek, and two others straightened her mismatched sweater, while the fourth adjusted her hair, which was done up in a thicket of braids, fine ones and fat ones, tangled and looped.

"Please be more specific." Robin led her toward the conference room for our initial intake meeting. "What's gone?"

"Everything! All the people on Elm Street—my whole neighborhood was erased, as if an exterminator teleported everyone away."

I cast a questioning glance at Sheyenne. "I'm not aware of any new teleportation services in the Quarter."

She shook her head. "No, and we review all the new postings in the Chamber of Commerce."

Mary slumped into a seat and rested her lower set of elbows on the conference room table while she placed her forehead in the other two palms. "I don't know what happened to everybody."

Robin pulled out a yellow legal tablet and sat across from the young woman. "We'll get to the bottom of this, Miss Celeste. Please, start from the beginning. When did you first suspect that your neighborhood had vanished?"

"When everyone disappeared! Just this morning I left my townhouse to get a bagel and coffee at the usual corner place. I'd had a, uh, late night and overslept—probably because the street was so quiet." Mary sniffled again. "When I stepped out the door, there were no cars on the street, no people on the sidewalk, no customers in the shops. A couple of bicycles lay abandoned in the streets. At the corner café, the burners were on, but nobody was inside. Music was playing on the transistor radio that the old werewolf vendor listens to at his newsstand."

"A transistor radio?" I asked. "That's very suspicious."

"Help me find my neighborhood," Mary pleaded. "Go see for yourselves."

For a thorough investigation, I try not to take the details for granted, so I felt obliged to ask, "Has your neighborhood ever disappeared before?"

"Not that I can recall. I think I would have noticed."

Robin contemplated the case, while her magic-powered pencil took detailed notes all by itself on her legal pad. The pencil and legal pad had been a gift from the actual Santa Claus, after we'd wrapped a case for him. "Why didn't you go to the police first?" she asked.

Mary looked lost. "On what basis? Is it illegal to vanish into thin air? I don't want to make my neighbors angry … but I'd like to know where they all went. They couldn't all have taken a vacation at the same time, could they? Or gone to the same shoe sale?"

Sheyenne's ectoplasmic light took on a cool tinge. "If your neighbors are missing through nefarious means, they will want to be found, no doubt. They may be willing to self-ransom and pay a finder's fee. Crowdfunding for missing persons."

I could see that the skittish Mary needed reassurance. "Don't worry, we're definitely going to find them. But the first step is we have to start looking."

SHEYENNE AND I escorted MARY OVER TO ELM STREET TO begin the investigation, while Robin and Alvina remained behind. The UQ Police Department dispatched Officer McGoohan to meet us at the scene. He was waiting for us at the corner when we arrived, ready to file a missing neighborhood report.

McGoo stood looking down Elm Street, which was nightmarishly quiet. He leaned toward me and spoke in a loud whisper, "Creepy all right, but not as creepy as where Stella Artois lives. I've got to tell you about it, Shamble."

"That librarian's been through a lot, so I wouldn't expect normal," I said. "Right now, I want to know what happened here." I looked down the street, the utter domestic emptiness weighed on me.

Sheyenne said, "It's like a ghost town, without the ghosts."

McGoo's brow furrowed. "I'm worried that a disintegrator field or teleportation service is still operating in the area. Do you think ghosts can be teleported?"

"Doubtful." On her own initiative, Sheyenne drifted down the street, and Mary hurried after her. When neither of them vanished, McGoo and I bravely followed.

A set of multifamily townhouses had dreary dark-shingled roofs and dreary dark shutters on the windows. Some of the lower levels had been converted into shops and home businesses with quaint signs: a spider creature with a grandmotherly head, advertising specialized embroidery; a garish neon sign in a window advertised "palm reader and backscratcher."

A brightly painted coffee and espresso cart was parked against a curb, decorated with multicolored Christmas lights looking festive and blinking, but no one was there to serve.

The breakfast place on the corner had a dining counter and a few tables and chairs outside. I smelled bacon. Doughnuts and bagels filled the display case. But nobody sat at the tables. No one stood behind the counter. The cash register was wide open.

Two bicycles lay in the street, as if their riders had simply vanished while pedaling along. A canvas messenger bag filled with folded copies of the morning newspaper lay sadly in the gutter.

"When exactly was the last time you saw anyone?" I asked Mary.

"I came home pretty late last night and didn't look at my watch." Embarrassed, she toyed with her elaborately entangled braids. "I was out dancing. I like to really get into it, move my body." She began to demonstrate, waving her torso back and forth, rippling her double pairs of arms in a hypnotic serpentine movement. "I, uh, had too much to drink, so when I got home, I just crawled into bed and crashed. This is the worst hangover ever."

Sheyenne asked, "So it's possible everyone had already vanished by the time you came home?"

"You must have been gone when the teleportation beam hit the whole street," McGoo said.

"Or when the shoe sale was announced," I offered, always open to possibilities.

CHAPTER 7

Mary Celeste went with McGoo down to the UQ police station to file a whole series of missing-persons reports. Meanwhile, as Sheyenne and I left the unnaturally quiet Elm Street, my thoughts were full of holes, just like the one in the middle of my forehead.

I'd solved other missing un-persons cases over the years, but in those cases, only a handful of monsters had disappeared at a time. This was a lot more extensive. How do you lose an entire neighborhood population overnight?

On our way back to the offices, Sheyenne suggested, "Maybe the landlord simply evicted the neighbors. All at once, just like that." She snapped her spectral fingers. "That's why you should always be a good tenant."

As we walked up to our brick building, I asked, "How could anyone not like us? We pay our rent on time."

When we entered, Renfeld was doing his rounds, shuffling along, burbling a melody that made sense only to him. I greeted the building super, and he raised a gray, spotted hand as if he were lifting a heavy object.

Sheyenne continued, "There's more to being good tenants. We haven't even introduced ourselves to the basement denizens yet. We should get to know our new neighbors."

I thought of the chambers below street level, units with direct walkouts to the sewer system. "They usually keep to themselves, but I'm always happy to make connections. You never know when somebody might be a handy resource."

When we entered the offices upstairs, Robin was in the conference room with a blocky-faced cyclops, one of her new clients, while her ensorcelled pencil took notes on the yellow legal pad. It was an interesting case: the poor cyclops had undergone discount LASIK surgery, which had left him with persistent double vision, so he wanted to file a medical malpractice suit.

In the main room, Alvina laughed as she watched cute spider videos on her phone. Seeing her, I decided to make our visit a family outing. "Come on, kid. We're going to the basement to meet the new neighbors."

Sheyenne rummaged through a file folder full of greeting cards, looking for one with a nice housewarming sentiment. She seemed in a quandary, though. "I'm not sure what to bring as a gift, Beaux. We don't know who's down there. Would it be best to get a bouquet of flowers? What if the tenants are plant monsters who might take that as an insult? Should I make a casserole? Or bring cookies? Maybe raw meat?"

Such considerations had never been a problem before the Big Uneasy. "Let's just bring a card. It's the thought that counts."

Not wanting to interrupt Robin in her cyclops consultation, I left her a note, and then Alvina, Sheyenne, and I headed down two flights of stairs to the dank sublevels of the office building. The aroma wafting through the sewer entrance made me wish we had brought flowers after all.

The office building had only three subterranean units, and we stopped at the first door. It was secured with a thick padlock and barricaded with two-by-fours nailed across the entrance. A string of garlic dangled above the door, and warding symbols had been painted on the door itself. A small card next to the apartment number said, "No Solicitors."

We decided to try the next unit instead. The second door was wide open, but not inviting. The interior was entirely black—not just because the lights were turned off, but *black* like a portal to some nether emptiness. A faint moaning came from deep within.

Alvina walked right up to the door. "Should I knock?"

"Let's move on to the third one," I suggested. When the hollow moaning sound grew louder, I hurried us along.

The last door had a professionally engraved business sign mounted below a brass knocker. "G. Latinous, Consulting."

This looked more promising.

Sheyenne carried the housewarming card, which we had all signed. (Alvina turned the dot over her "i" into a little hand-drawn heart.) The kid rattled the brass knocker, and we stood together, smiling and waiting.

From behind the door we heard a sloshing sound like a rock tumbler filled with used motor oil and gravel. "One moment please," came a stuffed-up nasal voice.

The knob twisted one way and another, as if the occupant had trouble grasping it. Finally, the door swung open to reveal a mound of green-brown slime, a quivering blob that looked like the result of a horrific accident in a gelatin factory.

The blob's voice burbled out of a mouth indentation. "How may I help you?"

"Mr. Latinous?" Sheyenne asked. "Or Ms.?"

The blob withdrew, rolling and glooping back to give us room to enter. "I'm an asexual species, so no worries about pronouns, though I identify as 'he.' Just call me G."

The unit was furnished with a few chairs, a desk, a credenza, and a kitchenette in back. Tasteful art prints hung on the walls, including the classic painting of zombie puppies playing poker, one of the best-known works of ghost artist Alvin Ricketts from his postmortem period. Ricketts had been a client of ours a long time ago.

My half-daughter bounded into the office. "Hi, I'm Alvina! We're your neighbors from upstairs."

I extended a hand. "Dan Chambeaux, private investigator, and this is our office manager, Sheyenne."

"We just came to introduce ourselves and welcome you to the building." Sheyenne held out the envelope, then realized G. would have trouble opening it, so she extracted the card for him. "Welcome to the neighborhood."

G. Latinous extruded a pseudopod that slurped around my hand. He had a firm grip. "I am composed of phlegm, mucous, slime—but not in a bad way," he explained.

"I've seen your name on the wall directory in the lobby. Chambeaux & Deyer Investigations, correct?"

"That's right. Come up and see us sometime," I said.

"Can you even climb stairs?" Alvina asked.

"I'm a little stiff on cold days, but I can roll up and down," G. said. "There are advantages to being amorphous."

Seeing all the stains on the floor, I could think of disadvantages, too.

"I'll make us some tea." G. oozed and blurped toward the kitchenette, where he used a pseudopod to switch on an electric kettle and retrieved a set of delicate porcelain teacups. "The office came fully furnished." He rummaged in the cupboard, opening one door after another. "I know I have teabags in here."

"It's really not necessary," I said.

"Do you have any children?" Alvina asked. "Any bloblets I can play with?"

G. Latinous extruded pseudopods and broke off parts of himself that jiggled and rolled across the floor, jumped over each other, and glommed back onto his body. "Sometimes, but I tend to keep everything together, one big happy family." He made a splurting noise. "Kids can be little snots, you know."

The sentient mucous oozed back into the main room. The greenish swirls of color on his body mass were hypnotic, like the drifting lumps in a lava lamp.

I looked around the sparsely furnished office. "The sign on your door says that you're a consultant. What exactly do you consult on?"

"I'm flexible, whatever the client needs. Consulting is an amorphous term." He puffed himself up, rising and reshaping his body mass. "But I'm not a slimeball, honest."

We stayed as long as Sheyenne considered socially acceptable, then Alvina gave a teasing poke to our squishy new neighbor and said goodbye. I politely took one of G.'s business cards. I didn't know when I might need someone with flexible ethics.

CHAPTER 8

That night we held a small celebration in the office for Big Uneasy Day. It was a prominent holiday in the Unnatural Quarter, with many street parties and heavily advertised "uneasy sale events."

Thirteen years ago the planets had aligned under a full moon. I thought of the *Necronomicon*, the virgin librarian, the shed blood ...

Robin, Sheyenne, and I didn't usually make a big deal of it, but since Alvina was with us now, we were always looking for excuses to have cake—red velvet cake, which was the kid's favorite. Sheyenne, who had ordered from a bakery down the street, proudly opened the box to display the words written in frosting: *13 Big Uneasy Years*.

Alvina sat on her chair, swiveling back and forth, as she leaned over the cake. Sheyenne brought out a stack of paper plates and napkins. I came from the kitchenette carrying a long knife.

Sheyenne said, "Such a shame that Stella became a recluse. Normally, such a celebrity would have held a huge party like New Year's Rockin' Eve. She's revered by unnaturals everywhere, no matter what sourpusses like the Olde Tymers say."

Well-versed in social media, Alvina explained, "No matter what you do, somebody complains. There are always trolls, and not just the ones that live under bridges." She gave some examples of blood-boiling comments that had been posted on her *I Was a Teenage Vampire* blog. "You just have to ignore them. Don't feed their negative energy."

She leaned forward on her chair, focused on the cake like a rattlesnake staring down a mouse. "Are you going to cut the cake, or just stand there with a threatening knife?"

I raised the blade and brought it down right through the middle of the word UNEASY.

A tentative but polite rap on the office door interrupted our celebration, and Mary Celeste entered, shivering. She clasped her lower two hands in a beseeching gesture, while the upper arms hung loose at her side. "I know it's after hours, but … do you mind?"

I looked at the clock on the wall: 11:30 PM. "We don't have posted office hours."

"You're welcome anytime, Ms. Celeste," Robin said.

"We have cake!" Alvina smiled. "Plenty for all of us."

Mary entered, hesitated, then used one of her hands to close the door behind her. "I spent the day down at police headquarters giving my statement." Her lower lip trembled. "I had to fill out missing-persons sheets, but I could only describe a dozen or so of my neighbors."

"We'll find them, Mary," I said, feeling a bit guilty, since I had no leads whatsoever. So far. But I would dig something up tomorrow, I was sure of it, once I applied my detective skills.

"Could I stay here a while? I just don't feel comfortable going back to Elm Street." She looked up, suddenly alarmed. "What if it happens to me? I could get body-snatched away tonight."

"That's a valid concern," Robin said.

Sheyenne gestured her toward the table. "Join the party. As Alvina said, we have plenty of cake."

I finished butchering the dessert, and the kid plopped messy pieces onto paper plates. We ate with plastic forks.

Mary gave a woeful sigh. "Unnaturals love to celebrate Big Uneasy Day, but I was just a normal six-year-old girl in a small town when I suddenly sprouted these extra arms." By way of demonstration she picked up another piece of cake, a napkin, and a second plastic fork, still leaving one hand free. She made expressive gestures as she told a story, while her other pair of hands went about serving herself bites of cake.

"My mother didn't know what to do with me. As a teenager I kept being accused of shoplifting and kleptomania. When I was fifteen, though, my dad got too handsy, and so I ran away from home." Mary shrugged, which was an awkward, caterpillar-like motion. "But we make the best of it, don't we? We have high hopes. We have dreams."

With one hand she dabbed frosting from the corner of her mouth. "As a normal small-town girl, I didn't have much chance for a career outside of the local chicken megafarm."

"You could be a magician," Alvina said, "or a juggler. Handy dandy."

"I prefer the term ambi-polydextrous," she said, and Robin made a note of it. "I knew I could make something of myself with these four hands. I wanted to become a star. There were more possibilities than I could count on all twenty fingers." She sounded breathless. "I came to the Unnatural Quarter so I could be ..." She drew out the moment. "A hand model!"

Mary set down her cake and spread her hands on the table. Seeing her beautiful nails, I imagined her with bottles of nail polish, files, cuticle boards, spending hours giving herself full manicures.

"I'm listed with several ad agencies and modeling sites, but I need my big break. The only job I've been able to get is a part-time gig at the Magic Fingers Massage, but it's a terrible place to work. To pay the bills, I wash dishes at the Ghoul's Diner, but dishwashing isn't good for my hands. I hope to move up."

Mary seemed noticeably more comfortable as she kept talking, and then she helped herself to a third piece of cake. Outside, fireworks and bottle rockets went off—or maybe gunshots, but I was being optimistic—as monsters celebrated.

Robin pulled up a chair at the table, and Sheyenne returned with a deck of cards. "We could play games."

Mary snatched the cards, cut the deck, and shuffled and spun out the cards in a blur, using all four hands like two professional Las Vegas blackjack dealers superimposed onto one. She shuffled again and fanned the rest of the deck. "Call the game."

"Poker," Alvina said right away, much too familiar with the subject. "Texas hold 'em."

We settled in to play cards.

CHAPTER 9

nniversaries are a time for reflection, and reflections remind me of funhouse mirrors—an appropriate metaphor, since I was thinking back to when all of reality became distorted.

The night of the Big Uneasy.

As Mary Celeste cut, shuffled, and cut the deck again to deal out another round of Texas hold 'em, Alvina scooped up her winnings. She batted her eyelashes to make us think she was just an innocent little girl, but no one believed it after she won three hands in a row.

I picked up my cards, but my thoughts were elsewhere.

Thirteen years ago ... a night to remember. Wasn't that the title of an old movie about the *Titanic*? That was an even better metaphor than a funhouse mirror.

It had seemed a perfectly normal night under a full moon—the world's last normal night. And "normal" for me was nothing to get excited about. I was a down-and-out private detective taking on lousy cases to pay the bills, regretting most of the jobs and perfectly happy to let the cases solve themselves. I had no real passion for my profession, not that the work warranted it.

Each time I took a case that was even less glamorous than the previous one, I had to deal with shrewish complaints from my wife Rhonda—and sometimes McGoo's wife Rhonda as well—about what a loser I was, not living up to my potential and certainly not meeting her expectations.

My Rhonda never let me forget that I'd washed out of the police academy and was forced to become a private investigator. She considered my best friend to be a stellar example of what a real man could be. Ironically, McGoo's Rhonda pointed to me as an example of a guy who was his own boss.

I couldn't win. Just like playing a game of poker with a four-armed card dealer.

On that fateful night, I was working a case I considered to be the rock bottom for my career. It was an ugly divorce case, a real dog in more ways than one. But the client had met my rigorous criteria—she paid half up front.

So, there I was out at midnight with my camera and my camouflage clothes, taking pictures of a mild-mannered, middle-aged man named Erwin Bush with a pet French bulldog. Peeping Toms get a thrill out of this sort of thing, but to me it was just a job, and a really shitty one at that.

The fat, snuffling French bulldog was an object of vitriolic dispute in the division of property between Ludmilla and Erwin Bush. Neither side had yet suggested the King Solomon solution of hiring a veterinarian to cut the bulldog in half, but considering Ludmilla's screed, and the fiery responses of her not-soon-enough-ex-husband Erwin, that option might be on the table soon.

My job was to lurk in the shadows and watch the man's behavior around the bulldog, with the goal of securing photographic proof that he was an unfit pet parent. I hated sneaking around, but I was getting good at it. I kept a logbook documenting how many times Erwin took the bulldog out for a walk, how many blocks he went, and how much affection he gave the animal.

Even worse, the man also had a big, gray cat. The two pets got along just fine, as far as I could tell, but I'd been hired to take photos proving that Erwin paid more attention to the cat than to the dog.

Under the light of the silvery moon, I wanted to howl in frustration.

I was in Erwin Bush's backyard creeping around with my penlight, pointing the beam at the ground and counting the piles of un-picked-up dog poop—some fresh, some old—to demonstrate the man's negligence. My job performance depended on the quantity of dog turds.

Yes, this was truly the low point of my private detective career.

The client wanted me to store poop samples in evidence bags to be presented in court, but I conveniently forgot that part of the assignment.

Then at midnight, while I was mourning my lost hopes and dreams, I felt an odd *snap* in the air, smelled a crackling energy like ozone. The bulldog began howling inside the house, and all the dogs in the neighborhood set up a similar chorus.

Up in the sky, the stars shimmered, shifted a little, and then snapped back into position. My guts twisted, like a callback from the bean burrito I'd had for lunch. With green-chile hot sauce. Lots of green chile.

I reeled, but caught my balance just before my knee squished a fresh treasure pile from the bulldog. I looked around, trying to figure out what had changed, but didn't see anything obvious.

The stars were back where they should have been. The full moon looked like a bright batsignal in the sky. A headache pounded in my skull, like the second day of a hangover following a real bender.

Lights flickered in all the houses on the street. The howling dogs subsided after about five minutes, and I began to convince myself that nothing unusual had happened after all. I turned on the flashlight again and bent down to count turd piles, when I saw my first werewolf.

It would be the first of many, but at the time I didn't realize that. I had no idea what I was looking at: a snarling, broad-shouldered man with fur busting out of his cheeks, eyebrows, and forehead. His face was elongated into a canine snout, with black lips and plenty of fangs. His hands/paws ended in long black claws.

The werewolf bounded closer to me, his golden eyes blazing. With a growl, he said, "What the hell?"

I yanked out my .38 from my jacket and backed away, careful not to trip, because of the fecal landmines in the grass. In retrospect, I know I would have needed to load the gun with silver bullets. We faced each other, tense and terrified. The werewolf seemed as confused as I was.

I said the first thing that popped into my mind. "Are you going to rip my throat out?"

The werewolf bristled, insulted. "Well … are you going to say that werewolves don't exist?"

"I'm a detective. I can see what's right before my eyes, so I'll concede that you exist."

Now that the dogs had stopped howling, I heard a new wave of chaos rippling along the street—cars honking, glass breaking, screams, growls—and that made the dogs start barking all over again.

Three insubstantial human figures flitted by like special-effects escapees from the Haunted Mansion ride at Disneyland. Their open mouths let out loud moans, but these spirits weren't in haunting mode, just baffled.

The specter of a bearded old man with hollow eye sockets and a gray tweed business suit drifted by. He floated close to my face, and I felt a tingle on my skin.

The shade of a matronly old woman whisked past him. "Follow the light!" she said. "Follow the light!"

The ghosts drifted like moths toward the streetlight on the corner.

Across the street, a putrid, gray-skinned figure shambled along in rotten clothes, poking into one mailbox after another.

The werewolf glanced from side to side, his pointed ears alert. Neither of us had the faintest idea what was happening.

Eventually, he introduced himself as Carlos, and I fumbled in my pocket to pull out one of my P.I. business cards. He squinted, studying the name, then looked around the nightmarish chaos of the streets.

He made the understatement of the year. "Something's not right here, Mr. Chambeaux."

CHAPTER 10

Our card game ended a few hours after midnight. Alvina won handily, which prompted Robin to suggest that we play Go Fish for our next game night.

Most of the red velvet cake had been eaten. Mary Celeste polished off four pieces, since she burned off so many calories moving those extra limbs. She said she was on a tight food budget while waiting for her big break and trying to live on a diner dishwasher's wages.

Robin yawned, which triggered a subsequent yawn from both Sheyenne and me.

Mary glanced around, forlorn. "I don't really feel comfortable going back to Elm Street. I might have nightmares."

"Nightmares can't hurt you," I said.

"Can she stay here?" Alvina asked. "Pleeeeeeease?"

I shook my head. Our office didn't have room for anyone to sleep, and my private apartment wasn't much more than a closet, considering I could sleep just leaning against a wall. McGoo's place was even worse.

I glanced at Robin. "But there's another option."

She and I both turned to Sheyenne, who controlled the petty-cash account. My ghost girlfriend understood, and she glowed with a firm decision. "Yes, let's get her a room where she can feel safe. I'll authorize the expense."

As Alvina put the cards away, I reached for my fedora. "The Motel Six Feet Under is a nice place," I lied. "Come on, Miss Celeste. It'll be like putting you into witness protection."

"But I didn't witness anything. Do I need protection?"

"We use the term broadly."

The ambi-polydextrous young woman had tears in her eyes as she followed me out the door. "I missed work at the diner yesterday, so I have to get to the morning shift. I don't want to lose my job."

Thinking about the Ghoul's Diner, I hoped she might have higher aspirations.

We climbed into the Pro Bono Mobile parked at the curb, and the doors creaked and the chassis sighed with the added weight. Leprous chunks of rust flaked off the lower body. I turned the key, and the engine sneezed, coughed, then vomited gray fumes from the exhaust pipe.

"Is this car safe?" Mary asked.

"We all have to take risks."

I shifted into gear, and the Ford Maverick rolled forward with all the speed and grace of a blind, cowardly foot soldier charging into battle.

After talking for hours during the poker game, the two of us sat in comfortable silence for a while. The engine noise would have drowned out most conversation anyway.

Eventually, I raised my voice and asked, "Do you ever think about going back to your small town? Family and friends?"

Two of Mary's hands pressed the sides of her cheeks in a *Home Alone* expression of horror. "No, never! I couldn't possibly become a famous hand model in a small town. I'd have to work in the chicken-processing plant, and because of my extra arms they'd expect twice the output from me. Drumsticks, wings, breasts, even tenders!" She shuddered. "Washing dishes at the diner is a better job than that ... until I get my big break."

We reached the Motel Six Feet Under and Conference Center, which specialized in seedy rooms. Weeds grew up through cracks in the asphalt lot. A parking place up front was reserved for the on-shift manager and another for the coroner's vehicle. A flickering neon light announced "ACANCY." Other signs advertised the perks: color TV, air-conditioning, free-range breakfast, and no hidden cameras.

Since a number of previous cases had brought me to this motel, I'd signed up for their loyalty club. I kept the punch card in my wallet next to my private investigator's license.

After I parked, Mary leaned forward and peered through the bug-spattered windshield. I was about to apologize for overpromising the charm of the place, reiterating that this was only temporary, and we would get her back home as soon as I solved the case of the missing neighborhood. But she cut me off with a happy sigh. "This is charming—so nostalgic! A place like this would be called a Resort where I grew up."

I recovered quickly. "Only the best for our clients." I switched off the engine, and it died with a sound of finality.

A bored vampire front desk clerk in her early twenties sat playing a game on her phone. She had straight brown hair and glasses (even though vampires usually get restored vision as a side effect of growing fangs). Her name plate said Shawna Biggs, Night Manager On Probation.

Shawna glanced at me, then at Mary Celeste's tight sweater and multiple arms. A knowing look came to her eyes. "Room by the hour? Bed or coffin?"

Mary clearly didn't know what the manager was implying.

I snapped, "What do you mean, a coffin? I'm a zombie, and zombies don't use coffins. And she is ... I don't know what she is, but she doesn't sleep in a coffin. I want a nice bed and a nice room—and one key. For her."

With an apathetic shrug, the vampire clerk rummaged in her pigeonholes and pulled out a key with a dangling plastic fob. Shawna Biggs had been quick to make the wrong assumption, but at least she didn't seem judgmental. "You can share, for all I care."

"I need a shower and a nap," Mary said.

After Shawna provided us with toothpaste and toothbrush, soap, shampoo, and other toiletries from the front desk supply, I escorted my client to her room. The door opened to a musty smell of old carpeting, old furniture, and old paint. Mary inspected the bed, the bathtub and its dripping shower, a bulky Zenith TV circa 1972, and the percolating coffeemaker next to the sink.

"It has air-conditioning," I said by way of apology, "and I bet that's a real color TV."

"And no hidden cameras," Mary pointed out. "It'll do just fine."

"Call if you need anything, and please don't disappear in the meantime. We're hard at work on the case."

The motel's ominous promise about no hidden cameras made me wonder if Elm Street had neighborhood-watch cameras, which might offer clues about where everyone had gone. I climbed back into the Pro Bono Mobile and considered getting another air freshener to dangle from the mirror.

When my phone rang, I held it up to my face and grimaced until the facial recognition kicked in.

It was Robin. "We have another errand to run, Dan. Howard Phillips Publishing wants us to perform a wellness check on Stella Artois."

"Has there been a threat on her life? The Olde Tymers?"

"No, but she's gone into recluse mode again. By contract, Stella has to autograph a thousand signature pages for the *Necronomicon* special edition. The publishing twins want us to make sure Ms. Artois is prepared for the task. Her wrist needs to be limber."

"A thousand autographs ..." At the other night's book-launch extravaganza, I had signed maybe a dozen of the Shamble & Die books.

"Well, she agreed to it, contractually," Robin said. "But she's quite the introvert and often needs to be encouraged."

"Text me the address, and I'll go see her," I said. "Or do you think a zombie appearing at her doorstep might scare her?"

"Good point," Robin said. "I'll come with you."

CHAPTER 11

As I coaxed and cursed the engine of the Pro Bono Mobile, several motel guests opened their doors and shook fists at me, because the noise was loud enough to wake the dead. Two zombies and a vampire proved the point.

When I finally got moving, I swung by the offices to pick up Robin (although with the temperamental vehicle, "lurched" is a more accurate word than "swung"). Outside, I honked to let her know I was there, but the blatting and popping engine drowned out the horn. As I waited at the curb, a banshee walked by plugging her ears and giving me a dirty look.

I felt guilty about disturbing the peace. I reached out to pat the console. Warning lights on the dashboard flickered on and off like a nightmarish videogame, and I had no idea which alerts were real and which were just spurious electronic faults that I could ignore. Out of caution, I ignored them all.

Robin emerged wearing a navy-blue blazer and professional slacks for visiting Stella Artois. She walked with a "don't mess with me" stride, carrying her leather briefcase. Sometimes just entering a courtroom was enough for Robin Deyer to intimidate the opposition.

She climbed into the passenger seat. "The car sounds funny, Dan."

"I'll turn the radio up so you don't have to hear it." The

classic rock station was playing AC/DC, which helped a great deal.

Over the din of the radio and the engine, Robin explained that she hadn't been able to get in touch with Stella Artois, so the celebrity librarian did not know we were coming. After McGoo's odd description, I was curious to see her house for myself. "We'll be there soon," I said.

But the car responded out of spite. The engine wheezed and sighed in a long death rattle, and the Pro Bono Mobile coasted to a halt in the middle of the street. I looked at the dashboard, no longer needing to choose among the indicator lights, because every one of them was lit.

I turned the key in the ignition again and again, like twisting a knife, but the grinding sound was like mocking laughter from under the hood.

"Not again," Robin said.

"At least it didn't happen during a heated car chase," I said. "Any idea what to do?"

"Move it out of traffic. That always works as a first step," she said. She had plenty of experience with the temperamental vehicle.

With the car in neutral, Robin and I got out on either side and pushed it out of traffic. Bits of rust dropped off onto the pavement like a blood-spatter pattern.

Robin set her briefcase on the hood and rummaged through business cards. "We have emergency roadside assistance. I'll call the towing service on the plan."

I was surprised. "We have a plan?"

"Sheyenne set up the account for Chambeaux & Deyer." She raised her eyebrows. "You have a card, too. Isn't it in your wallet?"

"I keep things like that in my office desk drawer."

Robin held up the contact card.

Towin' Owen, Specialty Service
Manual tows upon request.
"We'll come whenever you need us—even in broad daylight!"

After calling the number, Robin gave our details to the answering service and hung up, satisfied. "They'll be here in a jiffy." She paused. "Unfortunately, a jiffy isn't a legally defined term, so we'll just have to wait."

We leaned against the car and watched pedestrians walk by, some unnaturals and some humans, going about their daily business. The strangest one was a pouting human woman with a green mohawk, Egyptian-level mascara, black lipstick, and safety pins through her ears, as if the Big Uneasy had transported her from the heyday of punk rock. She slipped into a bridal shop with lacy white dresses designed for all sizes and configurations.

I placed my palm on the hood, which felt warm from its laboring engine. "This old car has served us well."

"I knew we needed to upgrade," Robin said. "But I didn't have the heart. We've been through so much together." She had bought it ten years before the Big Uneasy, when she was just a law student. Her parents were reasonably well-to-do, but they had made Robin secure her own transportation. When she'd shown them the falling-apart old eyesore, they had been horrified, but she was proud of what she'd gotten with her own money.

Now Robin leaned against the door. "So many miles and memories ... so many repairs along the way, so many quarts of oil, so many gallons of gas."

"Best car we've ever had," I said. Chambeaux & Deyer Investigations had never been able to afford anything else.

The tow truck rumbled up after considerably longer than a "jiffy." It was a big, loud diesel truck with an open flatbed, a crane, and a dangling hook that would have filled a robot serial killer with glee. The vehicle stopped in front of the Pro Bono Mobile, and the hook swung menacingly from the crane arm.

Towin' Owen lowered himself out of the cab, which had been expanded to accommodate his bulk. He was an ogre of significant size, with broad shoulders, enormous biceps, a head the size of a Cooper Mini, and eyebrows that could have served as feather dusters. A low-slung lip was like a deflated tire innertube, but it inflated as the ogre expanded his mouth in a big smile.

"Always happy to help a damsel in distress." He waggled his bushy eyebrows at Robin, then looked at me. "And a dude. What seems to be the problem?"

Since Robin was the lawyer, I let her explain in detail. "Our car broke down."

"That's right up my alley." Owen looked up and down the street. "Or boulevard. I'll have you out in a jiffy."

Since I already knew how long a "jiffy" was, I reset my expectations.

The big ogre reached into the truck cab and worked a set of controls that lowered the flatbed at an angle in front of Robin's poor, weary car. The diesel engine kept chugging, and the hydraulics made ominous groans.

I glanced at the burly hook swaying on its chain. "Be gentle. Rust is the only thing holding the car together."

Towin' Owen looked at the hook and laughed. "Oh, no need for that. It's mostly for show, and for little kids to swing on. I'll give you a manual lift. Best choice under these circumstances." He nodded to himself, considering. "Minimal extra charge."

Owen bent down at the front of the car, rattled the bumper. In this position, his oil-stained blue jeans slipped down, revealing the waistband of his tighty-whitey underwear along with his butt crack, which in the ogre's case was more of a chasm. I had seen many horrible things in the Unnatural Quarter, but this ranked near the top of the list.

"Here we go." Towin' Owen squatted lower, and his pants slid down another few inches. He nudged his shoulder under the front of the car, and with barely a groan he stood up, lifting the Pro Bono Mobile on his back. He easily placed it onto the flatbed, stepped back, and wiped his enormous hands on the thighs of his jeans. "Easy-peasy. A lot faster than hooking all the machinery up."

"That was a quick jiffy," Robin said, clearly relieved. "Much better than the previous jiffy."

Owen ambled back to the driver's side door. "You two can ride with me up front. Plenty of room." He pulled a clipboard off his dash and scanned the paperwork. "Order goes to one of my usual body shops. We'll be there in a jiffy."

"A fast jiffy or a slow jiffy?" I asked.

The big ogre pondered. "Never been asked that before. A medium jiffy."

"That'll be fine," Robin said. She climbed in and slid over to the middle of the bench seat. I rode shotgun. "So long as we take care of the Pro Bono Mobile."

CHAPTER 12

The ogre drove with one massive hand in a stranglehold on the steering wheel. After asking us what we did for a living, he cheerfully admitted that he'd never had reason to hire either a lawyer or a detective.

Owen bobbed his shaggy head back and forth, humming to himself. "This is my dream job, owning my own tow service, having my own receptionist." He thumped a palm down on the hard dashboard. "Owning my own truck! Owen owns his own —has a nice ring to it!"

"Why is this your dream job?" Robin asked.

The ogre's laugh sounded like a small explosion. "I like to lift heavy things, and I like to see people in distress. Bingo! Perfect job for me."

Owen grabbed the shift lever and rammed it home as he downshifted, and we entered the parking lot of the auto body shop. Rusty vehicles were piled in various states of destruction and disrepair against a sagging chain link fence.

The big billboard outside the parking lot showed a helpful gremlin with a pointy grin. WREX AUTO REPAIRS. Three wide doors were open to cavernous repair bays from which wafted a racket of clanging, whirring, and banging, along with the high-pitched chittering of unnatural voices.

"You'll like these guys," Owen said. The diesel engine let out a loud disbelieving hiss as he ground the truck to a halt. "They're certified."

He climbed out of the truck and trudged back to the flatbed, where he wrapped his arms around the Pro Bono Mobile, heaved it off the truck, and set it down with a crash in the guest parking zone. Towin' Owen snagged a clipboard from the cab and had us sign the service form. With a sausage-like finger, he pointed to the main building. "Go see Wrex in the front office."

Robin and I headed toward the repair shop. Inside, the walls were covered with dark wood paneling like a basement man cave from a 1970s sitcom. On the low front desk, an old computer terminal sat next to a three-ring binder. Pens and pencils were scattered all over the countertop, which barely came up to my waist, and wads of paper had been thrown at a wastebasket on the floor, most of them missing the target.

The gremlin manager—Wrex, I presumed—had a face full of gray fur, needle-sharp teeth, large eyes that could have been sad or terrifying, and pointed ears that flopped or drooped as his attention wandered. A big bowl on the counter held an assortment of mismatched and unmarked car keys, like leftovers from an automotive swingers party.

The gremlin's fanlike ears perked up, and he asked in a raspy but polite voice, "Need some damage? Do you have an appointment?"

"Our company vehicle was just brought in by Towin' Owen." Robin pulled out her emergency roadside service card. "We have the premium membership, and we need the car serviced as soon as possible. Our business depends on it."

The gremlin inspected the roadside service card. "I have the best team of gremlin mechanics who can either install or remove repairs, per the customer's wishes."

I dropped the car key into the bowl with all of the other single and lonely vehicles. "It's a 1972 Ford Maverick."

Wrex typed in the information on his monitor. "Color?"

"Lime green," Robin said.

I added, "With rust-colored highlights."

The gremlin turned to a wall calendar that featured a scandalously buxom reptilian swimsuit model. "We have a full schedule. Lots of people want their cars wrexed."

"We'd like our car *fixed* please," Robin said.

The gremlin made a note. "Similar process, different end result." He picked up one of the loose pencils from his countertop, thrust it into his mouth, and gnawed it with his pointy teeth. "Could take a week or two." When he looked up, his ears drooped, then popped up again. "Let me talk to the boys in the shop." He bounced off his swiveling stool and dropped to the floor. He pattered to the door leading into the repair bays, motioning for us to follow.

Loud music boomed in the repair bay, overshadowed by a symphony of jackhammers, hydraulic lifts, and other power tools. A crowbar clanged on the concrete floor. A furry gremlin ducked into the vault beneath a hydraulic lift and clambered under a car. Using his claws, he ripped out wires and hoses, casting them aside like entrails.

Another gremlin hung by one hand from a chain on the ceiling, hooting as he scattered rusty bolts across the bay. A third gremlin inspected a beautiful, jet-black Ferrari, raised a sledgehammer over his head, and brought it crashing down on the highly waxed hood.

Wrex nodded with pride as the gremlin took a second heavy swing, smashing the front grill this time. "He's installing dents. Best in the business! These are my guys—Winkin, Blinkin, and Todd."

Wrex whistled for the three gremlins to pause in their work. The third gremlin rested his sledgehammer on the floor, while the one dangling from the ceiling chain waved at us. The first gremlin poked his head above the edge of the vault, showing only his eyes.

"These people are having trouble with their car," Wrex said. "Towin' Owen delivered it."

"Owen's a good guy," said the gremlin named Todd. "Brings us lots of business."

Blinkin said, "Careful he doesn't overcharge you for his manual lift."

"We'll look over the paperwork," Robin said.

"How soon can we take a look at their vehicle?" Wrex inquired. "Can you squeeze it in?"

"Just squeeze it? Or do they want it totaled?" Winkin raised his sledgehammer, waggled it, and nodded toward the damage he had done to the black Ferrari.

"No," Robin and I said in unison.

"Check the reconstruction calendar then, instead of the destruction calendar." Todd ducked back under the car on the lift and continued to pull out wires and hoses.

"The car has great sentimental value," I said, looking at Robin. "And a lot of mileage. This isn't her first trip around the odometer."

"We specialize in lost causes," said Wrex. "Carry on, boys." He gestured to the trio of mechanics. "They really are good at what they do—I hired all three from the airport. They used to work on big jet engines."

Glancing at her watch, Robin gave me a worried look. "We'll need a loaner vehicle in the meantime. It's covered on our premium plan."

Wrex brightened. "Anything for our premium customers.

We have one loaner vehicle left. First class. Top of the line. It's a limo."

We followed him out to the back lot, where all the vehicles visible were sagging rust heaps on cinderblocks, or dismantled into spare doors, chassis, axles, hubcaps. Wrex grabbed a gray tarp covering a long vehicle and yanked it away with a flourish to reveal a black hearse with faded paint and a loose emblem in the back. The black vinyl ragtop was scuffed and frayed.

"That's a hearse, not a limo," I pointed out.

Wrex shrugged. "Classification categories were expanded after the Big Uneasy, and the aftermarket demand has been extreme. Can't find one of these babies at any car lot in the Quarter!"

Robin's mouth was set in a firm line. "We'll take it. We have business to conduct."

To my chagrin, the hearse/limo completely outclassed our puttering old Pro Bono Mobile. When I used the keys that Wrex the gremlin handed me, the engine started up like a charm.

It was time to head off to our late unexpected surprise visit with Stella Artois.

CHAPTER 13

Because of her deep desire for privacy, the celebrity librarian lived in a gated, and moated, community on the other side of town. In our loaner hearse, I drove at the speed of a double-time funeral procession, and before long we made it to the guard gate.

In a security kiosk just outside the main entrance, a heavyset zombie wore a slack expression. I pulled up next to the kiosk and rolled down the hearse's window, but I had to honk the horn to get the zombie's attention. His name badge said DONALD.

He gave me a long stare before he finally managed, "Help you?"

Impatient because we were late for our unscheduled appointment, Robin leaned over the seat. "Dan Chambeaux and Robin Deyer to see Ms. Stella Artois."

I added, "On behalf of Howard Phillips Publishing." Given all the time he sat around in the guard shack, maybe Donald was a big reader.

The zombie guard leaned back in his chair for such a long moment I thought he'd forgotten we were there. Finally, he picked up his clipboard and studied the names written there, mouthing each one phonetically, then shook his head. He held out the clipboard to me. "Not on list."

"Let me see that." I took the clipboard, removed the pen

stuck to the top, and wrote my name and Robin's at the bottom. I handed it back to him. "There we are. You can let us in now."

Donald squinted at the names, then nodded. "Sorry. Must have missed it."

He pulled a lever. Engines hummed, gears and drums turned, a cable spun tight, and the big imposing gate creaked open.

I shifted the hearse into gear and rolled forward to the edge of a deep moat filled with both sharks and crocodiles, which seemed like twice as much security as necessary. The engine idled, and we waited again as a drawbridge groaned and squeaked into place.

At last, we drove into a pleasant tree-lined housing development. The houses were all built along the same basic model, early Addams Family, and would look like proper haunted houses after a century or so of neglect and decrepitude. The curved lanes and cul-de-sacs were not organized in any recognizable fashion, and I had forgotten to ask Donald for a map, but I was good at wandering. I found the right address by trial and error.

Stella's home was set apart from the others, a well-maintained nouveau Victorian with a fresh coat of paint and neatly trimmed barrier hedges.

Robin and I went up the sidewalk toward the front porch. The walk was lined with rusty barbed wire rather than flowerbeds. Signs posted in the yard warned KEEP OUT and NO TRESPASSING. In the middle of the lawn another sign said WARNING: MINE FIELD.

"Stella likes her privacy," I said.

Robin nodded. "Over the years, she's suffered constant

harassment and unsavory attacks by internet trolls and real-world trolls."

We climbed the wooden steps to the covered porch. No doubt, Stella had an array of security cameras watching us. I adjusted the fedora to cast a shadow over my forehead bullet hole. With her briefcase at her side, Robin stepped up to the front door and pushed the button under a little handwritten card that said "Do Not Ring Bell." Tinny electronic Westminster chimes rang throughout the house.

Given all the threatening signs and ominous warnings, I feared some trapdoor might drop out from under our feet so we'd plunge into a spike-filled pit beneath the porch. If that happened, I'd try to protect Robin by falling first. That way I could try to cover the spikes and save her, though I admit that wasn't the best of all possible plans.

Rather than shrieking alarms, spring-loaded shotguns, or other automated defenses, we heard quiet footsteps approach. After the lock clicked, the front door opened to reveal the shy librarian with her round, wire-rimmed glasses and a drab housedress. "Oh, you must be from Howard Phillips Publishing. Donald at the gate called to let me know you were on your way."

Robin tucked her leather case under her arm and introduced us. I extended my hand. "We met briefly the other night, ma'am."

"Yes, of course, you were at the table beside me during the book signing." She seemed more warm and friendly in this casual setting, without a huge crowd. "You write novels. I'm glad to meet someone who loves books."

"We don't actually write them, but we're in them," I said. "Or at least a fictionalized version of us."

"Every book is a fictionalized version of something." Stella stepped back to let us enter. "Otherwise it wouldn't be fiction."

Standing close to the librarian, I felt a tingle of fanboy excitement. "I admire your work, Ms. Artois. In fact, you changed my life."

She regarded my gray skin, the zombie shadows under my eyes. "I suppose I did." She sounded disappointed.

Following Stella down the long front hall, Robin said, "Howard and Philip Phillips asked us to make sure you're all right, after the awkwardness with the protesters at the gala."

The librarian's expression soured. "The Olde Tymers blame me for the Big Uneasy. As if I would have done such a thing on purpose!" Stella clucked her tongue. "But I never make political statements in public. How can they assume what I feel about the matter? They've never asked my opinion—I might agree with them, for all they know."

"I think it's best if you don't speak with them at all," Robin suggested.

"Also," I interjected, "the publisher will soon be delivering the stack of signature pages that you agreed to autograph. There is a tight turnaround with their *Necronomicon* production schedule, since it's already a year late."

Stella sighed. "I knew that was coming."

We stopped in the main reading room, where a roaring fireplace shed a warm, homey glow. Along the walls and in every corner sat elaborate Victorian dollhouses, meticulously rendered, each one painted a different color. A display case against the wall held numerous dolls, propped in uncomfortable-looking positions.

Two overstuffed leather reading chairs sat in front of the crackling flames, and a display table between the two chairs held a perfect model of the very room we were in. I bent over to look through the walls of the transparent protective case. The model included small versions of the reading chairs, as well as a perfectly accurate six-inch doll of Stella Artois herself, wearing a similar housedress, comfortably positioned with a tiny book in her lap. The doll faced a miniature fireplace where copper foil simulated the flames.

Seeing my interest, Stella smiled with pride. "I made that myself, a perfect likeness. It takes a great deal of patience, a steady hand, and fine-tipped paintbrushes." The librarian brushed an imaginary fleck of dust off the display case. "My miniatures are a reminder of a perfect world."

Stella motioned for us to follow her down the cluttered main hall. Even with my dulled sense of smell, I could tell the air was thick with musty paper and mold.

Though it was only a decade or so old, Stella's home had accumulated a century's worth of belongings. Deeper in the house, the walls and halls were lined with bookshelves stacked with paperbacks, hardcovers, and magazines. Cardboard boxes were full of newspapers yellowed with age.

A side room held crates of toys and action figures, all unopened and in pristine condition. Overburdened shelves contained packs of trading cards, commemorative plates, souvenir spoons. One section held metal lunchboxes from the 1960s.

"She's a hoarder," I whispered to Robin.

Stella overheard me. "I prefer the term *accumulator*. I'm a collector of things that interest me." She smiled. "Especially books. I was a librarian, you know. I love to read, and I love to *have* books." She pressed a hand against her heart. "Every character in every book helps me rebuild a normal, peaceful, and nostalgic world."

We reached the formal dining room, where an enormous

table could have served dozens of guests, if Stella Artois ever held parties. Instead of serving its intended purpose, though, the table displayed even more elaborate model kits and miniature figures.

"I collect and build these little showpieces. It fills me with warmth and happiness."

The last third of the cluttered dining table was empty, as if waiting for something. Stella explained, "I'm expecting a small model train set. I'll build a whole depot right here."

A set of large pocket doors on the far end of the dining room led to some other part of the house, but the doors were closed, the handles wrapped with a chain and padlocked.

I asked the polite question, "What's in there?"

"Just my craft room. I keep it closed for safety reasons. The paint thinner and X-Acto knives can be quite a hazard."

"Who are you worried about protecting in an empty house?" I asked.

"Oh, I'm not really alone." She nodded to the dollhouses, the miniature figures. "I'm filled with company—the company I choose and the company I keep. I don't even like to go outside because of my notoriety. I have to disguise myself with sunglasses and a big floppy hat." She drew a wistful breath. "Especially when I go to my beloved library."

Her cheeks flushed, as if an old wound had reopened. "I hate all the attention! I hate the paparazzi. I hate the screaming crowds of unnaturals who want my autograph, who want to kiss me, who want to ..." She looked away. "If only I'd had that sort of romantic attention before the fateful night, then none of this would have—"

When her eyes blazed, I heard a staccato slamming of doors throughout the house, loud cracks like gunshots.

Stella let out an embarrassed chuckle. "Oh my, too many

drafts in this place!" She calmed herself with a visible effort. "My closest friends were books. I could sit for hours and enjoy stories about Frankenstein, Dracula, Dr. Jekyll and Mr. Hyde." She sniffed. "But it's not the same now that they're all real! I can never go back to my quiet job, never go back to my old life, although I sometimes sit in the main library branch and reminisce, just like a normal patron ..."

Stella grew quiet, and her shoulders stiffened, as if she suddenly remembered that she didn't like company. She turned about and ushered us back to the front door. "That's all I wanted to show you. As you can see, I'm perfectly fine." She shooed us faster. "Tell Howard and Philip that I have my signing pen ready as soon as they send over the signature pages."

CHAPTER 14

Any bad day ends better when it ends at the Goblin Tavern. In fact, even a good day ends better when I can slump onto my usual barstool, have a cheap draft beer or two, and discuss the state of the world with my best human friend.

And that usually gets us depressed enough to order yet another round.

The tavern was a perfect watering hole for both humans and unnaturals, and the owners considered "dark, dingy, and sinister" a selling point. Nocturnal dwellers came for the ambiance. Tourists came for the extensive menu of martini potions broken down by species, some marked with asterisks for the more adventurous bev-curious.

After the original goblin owner sold the tavern, a new franchise tried to make it into a family-friendly establishment, adding brighter mood lights, replacing the ash wood pool cues with plastic rods to pose less danger to vampire customers. The TVs played a selection of classic movies, truly great cinematic works like *War of the Gargantuas* and *Abbott and Costello Meet Frankenstein*. The weekly trivia night was also a draw.

McGoo and I sat on our stools with elbows propped on the sticky bar surface, while keeping an eye on Alvina who amused herself at the dartboard. We had ordered her a bubbly red Shirley Jugular, which Francine the bartender made just for kids. At one time you weren't likely to find children in the Goblin Tavern, certainly not little girls, especially not little vampire girls.

At one time you wouldn't have found vampires or monsters here either.

Things change.

Alvina slurped her sweet scarlet drink through a straw and picked up a handful of darts. She flashed a smile at me, or maybe at McGoo, and hurled all five darts. The pointed missiles thunked into the dartboard in rapid-fire succession, hitting very close to the bullseye.

"That's my girl," McGoo said.

"She gets her depth perception from me," I said.

Alvina retrieved the darts. "You know you can get a videogame version of throwing darts. It's easier to play. I can download the app right now."

"Then you throw your phone at the dartboard?" I didn't understand the concept.

She rolled her eyes but didn't deign to respond.

McGoo leaned closer to me and lowered his voice. "Do you really think Al's okay? That postcard came out of nowhere today. I think it shook her up."

We watched Alvina take her position again, screwing up her expression as she concentrated on the dartboard.

"Rhonda sucks," I said.

McGoo snorted. "Understatement. The parenting books suggest maintaining some kind of contact with the birth mother, but I just don't see how any interaction with Rhonda benefits her."

I was surprised by that. "You read parenting books, McGoo?"

"I skimmed the book descriptions online."

I reached into my pocket and pulled out the postcard that had arrived at Chambeaux & Deyer that afternoon. If Sheyenne had noticed it among the incoming mail, she would have thrown it away, or maybe set fire to it. Instead, Alvina was helping sort through the junk mail and came upon it first.

McGoo happened to be in the office hanging around. When he was bored, he often came to see Alvina or to ask for advice on his cases. He'd been telling me a joke that I didn't want to hear when Alvina pulled out the postcard. Her already pale vampire skin went even whiter.

The postcard was addressed to Alvina.

From Rhonda.

"Happy Birthday little girl! I hope you're having fun.—Love, Mom."

I plucked the card out of the girl's hands and flipped it over to see a picture of city buildings. *Greetings from Dayton, Ohio.*

McGoo took it, and his expression turned to vinegar. "She's living it up."

"She remembered my birthday," Alvina said, "but it was six months ago."

McGoo tried to make light of it, for the kid's sake. "Maybe she's six months early for next year and didn't want to forget."

Alvina said, "Yeah, my mom likes to cover the bases because she loses track."

McGoo patted her on the shoulder. "You're daddy's little girl anyway."

Pretending not to care, she had dismissively tossed the card on Sheyenne's desk. "I like being with all of you. This is where I belong."

"Yes it is, honey." Sheyenne had hovered close to her. "Let's go see if there's any red velvet cake left in the fridge."

But we could all see that the kid's mood had been shaken....

Now, as we relaxed in the tavern late at night, Francine came in from the back room carrying a case of wine bottles and vodka, which she set heavily on the bar. Wiping her calloused hands on a rag, she scanned the room like a predator searching for customers in need of a drink.

I caught her attention. "Two more beers, Francine. And another Shirley Jugular for the kid."

Alvina hurled another fusillade of darts at the board, coming even closer to the bullseye. The girl snagged her drink, stuck the straw between her fangs, and slurped the rest of the bright liquid. She placed the empty glass in front of Francine.

The crusty old bartender chuckled. "We'll make a cocktail waitress out of you yet, squirt!"

Alvina beamed. "Thanks, but I haven't made any career choices yet. I just want something that doesn't suck."

Francine had worked at the Goblin Tavern ever since it was a dirtball human tavern. Her voice was raspy from breathing decades of cigarette smoke thick enough to have set off crematorium alarms. Layers of makeup were all that held her expression together. She'd had a hard life, more marriages than I remembered, and a disposition that allowed her to beat up drunken sailors and sober werewolves.

Francine had taken a liking to our little vampire girl, though. Her hard, shriveled heart had softened in recent months, now that she'd gone sweet on an old vampire gentleman who came in to flirt with her at the tavern. Old One Fang was a dapper, soft-spoken vampire, and he genuinely seemed to enjoy the bartender's company.

It was an unlikely relationship, but who am I to say? My own girlfriend is a ghost, and I'm a zombie. Sometimes love conquers all.

Francine set fresh beers in front of us. McGoo and I clinked our glasses together and sipped in unison. "Alvina's resilient," I said. "And she's smart. Someday she might even be running the Unnatural Quarter."

"That reminds me," McGoo said, as if he'd been waiting for a pause in the conversation. "What do sea monsters eat?"

"Fish and ships!" Alvina said.

"At least it wasn't a zombie joke," I muttered.

In a shadowy booth in the back of the bar, I noticed a frumpy woman sitting by herself, paging through manila folders, jotting notes on a spiral notepad. I recognized Linda Bullwer, better known as Penny Dreadful, and I assumed she was watching me on the sly, taking notes for the next Shamble & Die novel. That was puzzling, though. She had no need to be sneaky about it, since we had agreed to share parts of our real cases as inspiration.

Seeing Linda, I decided that talking to a vampire ghostwriter was better than risking another one of McGoo's jokes. I slid off the stool and took my beer over to her booth.

She had barely touched the martini in front of her. A long toothpick dangled in the murky gin, with two pickled eyeballs on the skewer.

"Hello, Ms. Bullwer," I said. "Do you come to the Goblin Tavern for inspiration? We're just starting a particularly interesting case, the mystery of a missing neighborhood."

"Oh, the readers love your cases, Mr. Shamble." She took a small sip from her martini, then lifted the toothpick and slurped one of the small eyeballs into her mouth. "I eagerly await whatever new escapades you and Ms. Deyer come up with."

McGoo joined us and stood beside the booth with his beer. "It's not just the adventures of Dan Shamble, ma'am. Don't forget his handsome best friend."

She made a quick note and slid the papers into the manila folders and tucked them away, as if afraid we might look at them. "Right now I have another project, completely hush-hush. My biggest contract yet!"

"More ghostwriting?" I asked.

"My name will not appear on the cover, not even my nom de plume, but this will be significant literature." She dabbed at her lipsticked mouth with a cocktail napkin. "I can always work on lightweight fluff like the Shamble & Die mysteries when I need a break."

McGoo chuckled. "Lightweight fluff, Shamble!"

"You're a lot heavier than I am," I said, then nodded to the vampire ghostwriter. "Whatever it is, we look forward to reading it, Ms. Bullwer."

"I'll wait for the audiobook," McGoo said.

We left her alone and decided to play a round of darts with Alvina, though McGoo didn't need any practice throwing barbs.

CHAPTER 15

McGoo and I set a good example for Alvina by leaving the Goblin Tavern well before last call, although "last call" is difficult to define with all the nightlife, day life, and un-life among the unnaturals.

Alvina beat us in two games of darts, but then McGoo pricked his thumb and bled all over a cocktail napkin, which drew altogether too much attention from some of the unsavory customers. We decided to head back home and put the kid to bed before sunrise.

"I've got a book," Alvina said. "When we get home, I can lie back and read for a while before I close the lid." She would probably take a flashlight and keep reading long afterward, too. It's hard to be a stern parent when you have such a good child.

When Alvina came to stay with us, McGoo and I went overboard to make proper accommodations, looking through undertakers' catalogs, shopping for sales on the best mahogany caskets. One company even had a special juvenile line upholstered with colorful Marvel characters or Disney princesses.

Since she had been turned into a vampire during a botched blood transfusion, rather than the usual method, Alvina had her own tastes. The elegant woodgrain finish and polished brass–handled models didn't interest her. Being a kid, she was more delighted by a large cardboard box from a new air-conditioning unit that Renfeld had installed. The first time she climbed inside and pulled down the cardboard lid, she called out in a muffled voice, "This doesn't suck at all. It's really comfortable!" We added blankets and a special pillow, and Robin brought her some stuffed animals. Best bed ever.

Seeing how much the kid loved the cardboard box, McGoo drove around the Quarter searching behind appliance stores until he found another big cardboard box for her to use when she stayed at his place.

Now, leaving the Goblin Tavern, we walked along under the streetlights. A pair of zombies in jumpsuits shoved push brooms along the gutters. A poltergeist pizza-delivery guy flitted past us close enough that we could smell the savory cheese and pepperoni. A retired gargoyle couple sat out on lawn chairs just watching the world go by. Someone let out a bloodcurdling shriek down an alley, but it sounded like a good-natured shriek followed by ghoulish laughter, so we walked on.

Everything seemed normal, or as close as it was going to get.

McGoo's brow furrowed in contemplation, which in itself was cause for concern. It's not good when he thinks too much.

"Everything's so quiet and calm, Shamble. Who would have thought? Remember that first night? After the Big Uneasy, the world went to hell in a handbasket. Or a dump truck."

"How could I forget?"

"Well, you do have a hole in your head."

Alvina skipped along beside us. "I learned all about the Big Uneasy in school."

For all of the kid's life, monsters had been *real*, rather than imaginary legends or chilling ghost stories. Most unnaturals were okay, many of them quite friendly. In fact, the real boogeyman was a well-respected entrepreneur selling life and afterlife insurance.

That first night, though, had been total chaos.

I recalled Carlos, my first werewolf on my night of counting bulldog turds for Ludmilla Bush's divorce case. Since I had no answers for the hairy guy, he howled at the moon in frustration.

I tried to be reasonable. "There's a lot of crazy stuff going on, Carlos. Just take a breath. Don't panic."

As if to contradict me, a banshee's scream shattered the night, along with several windows. Carlos's bristly fur stood on end. "What am I going to do-o-o-o-o-o-o-o?" He drew out the last word into a howl. He wiped a paw across his muzzle and smeared the saliva that had drooled down his jaw. "You've got to help me."

The thought of me protecting this enormous lycanthrope seemed silly. "Just find a quiet place and wait this one out. Everything will look better in the morning."

I made sure he had my business card. *Dan Chambeaux, Private Investigator. Wide range of services.* "The world's not going to end. It can't be all that bad."

Carlos fumbled the business card with his paw. "All right, Mr. Chambeaux, I won't overreact." He pocketed the card in his torn pants, then loped off into the night.

The banshee shrieked again, which made the French bulldog and the neighboring dogs set up a counterpoint racket. I felt a new resolve: counting turds was not my priority anymore. Even though I had tried to reassure Carlos, the world might well be coming to an end after all....

LIFE GOT CRAZIER OVER THE NEXT SEVERAL DAYS. MISTY SPIRITS swirled around cemetery plots like a ghost-a-palooza, exchanging centuries worth of gossip. Poltergeists acted out every imaginable teenage prank, drifting up behind pedestrians to give them wedgies, while others rang doorbells and disappeared like a whisp of fog. Hungry monsters chased people up and down the streets—or maybe they were just frisky.

Homeowners formed militias to defend their property with pointed wooden sticks and defiant crosses. Fierce advocates of property rights, they stood on their front porches and threatened unnaturals who were just looking for a place to hide before sunup. Waving a sharpened garden stake, one old man menaced a skittish vampire who had crawled into the thick shade of his hedge before dawn. "Get off my lawn!"

During those crazy times, McGoo was on the job patrolling the streets, but not sure what to do. All police had been called out, promised overtime, and I helped him defend the endangered people. We were both exhausted and tense, but McGoo braced himself. "We do what we have to do. It's all part of the job description."

I blinked at him. "Where does the job description say that we're supposed to fight monsters?"

Besides, it wasn't my "job description" in any way, shape, or form, because I wasn't even a cop. Washed out. At the time that failure had seemed important. Our test scores weren't all that different, but I'd missed the cutoff by a few points, and McGoo had barely made it by the same margin. Not much difference, and yet a crucial difference.

When I'd told my friend I was going to be a P.I., he nodded knowingly. "Remember that old cliché—those who can't do, teach? Well, it's kind of the same situation. Those who can't be cops, become private detectives."

I felt defensive. "Haven't you seen TV? Private investigators are romantic heroes, sympathetic characters, sexy and brooding. Everyone roots for them. Just look at all the P.I. shows on TV."

McGoo had countered, "Oh? Think of all the cop shows. *We're* the romantic heroes."

We had then rushed off to count programs—private investigator shows and cop shows—throughout the history of television.

Yeah, we had a different set of priorities then.

McGoo worked shift after shift just trying to keep some semblance of order in the city, and also to prevent monster murders—murders by monsters, and murders *of* monsters. We were taken aback when terrified unnaturals came to us begging for help against predatory humans. I didn't know what services a private detective could offer them.

That was before I'd met Robin Deyer....

Just dealing with the aftermath of what became known as the Big Uneasy was more than a full-time job. My Rhonda complained every time I came home late, saying I was too busy with work to pay any attention to her ... even though she could see the chaos sweeping across the world. I was fighting monsters. She wanted someone to do the dishes.

McGoo commiserated with me, because *his* Rhonda complained about the same thing every night when he got home.

Now as we walked Alvina back home from the tavern, the reminiscing unsettled me. I shook my head and muttered, "What a disaster."

McGoo pressed his lips together. "Yeah, the Big Uneasy sure caused a mess."

I looked down at the little vampire girl and lowered my voice. I touched the postcard in my pocket. "No, I meant Rhonda."

CHAPTER 16

After thirteen years in the Unnatural Quarter, we had gotten rather blasé about seeing mythical creatures in everyday life. But the client who walked into our office the next day was a real legend.

Hairy Harry, the rogue werewolf cop.

The door slammed open, because the angry lycanthrope couldn't control his temper or his strength. I hurried out of my office, assuming that any loud, unexpected noise had to be more interesting than the old paperwork on my desk.

Hairy Harry shifted his gaze back and forth, as if he was afraid of being ambushed. A growl came from deep within his throat.

Sheyenne's voice was bright and welcoming. "Hello again, Mr. Harry." He had been a client of ours once before.

Hairy Harry was big and hirsute, dark-furred with a flash of gray at the temples. He wore a rumpled tweed jacket and an untucked checkered shirt. Despite his disheveled appearance, I could see that he had actually gotten dressed up for this meeting. He carried two books tucked under his elbow.

I approached him with my hand extended. "Has your hellhound gone missing again? We can solve the case a second time, if necessary."

The werewolf cop's tongue lolled from the side of his muzzle. "Oh, Lucky's just fine, bigger than ever. He's grown into that spiked collar, but he's a real pawful, keeps running into the street and chasing cars."

"I hope he doesn't get hurt," Sheyenne said.

"Him?" Hairy Harry growled. "I'm worried about the insurance on all the vehicles he wrecks."

The werewolf cop had hired us to rescue his rambunctious hellhound puppy from a radical animal rights group called GETA, Gremlins for the Ethical Treatment of Animals. They had taken desperate measures to prevent Lucky from being neutered, but when Hairy Harry got his pet back, the balls were in his court.

Now he clicked the lock on the office door. "For privacy." He glanced around like a hunted animal. "I'm here on an entirely different matter, punk. Nothing to do with Lucky this time."

Alvina was at the table, busy with homeschooling workbooks that Robin had given her, working her way though a complex textbook called *Estate Law for Children*. Now she trotted up to greet the curmudgeon werewolf. "Are you really Hairy Harry? Do you carry a .44 Magnum filled with silver bullets?"

He lifted his tweed jacket to reveal the enormous holstered handgun. "Right here." He chuffed, and I could see he was a bit starstruck himself. "And is it really you? Alvina? From the *I Was a Teenage Vampire* blog?"

I stepped closer to my half-daughter. "What does the kid have to do with this?"

Hairy Harry snarled at me, "Nothing to do with you, punk!" His tone made my cold skin crawl, but he was only interested in my half-daughter. "I'm a big fan, girl. I follow you on Monstagram."

She giggled. "Really?"

Robin poked her head out of her office, but Hairy Harry dismissed us all. "Not here to see any of you—this is a case for a social-media influencer." He slapped the two books on the table next to Alvina's homework. I could see they were both the same.

Make My Day: Memoirs of a Rogue Werewolf Cop.

The cover art was garish and poorly executed, as if drawn by someone who'd been encouraged to enter an art talent contest by a nearsighted grandmother. The designer had managed to put five different fonts on the front cover.

Alvina picked up a copy. "Ooh, I like to read."

The back cover had an old photo of Hairy Harry, from when he still wore his UQPD police uniform.

"I poured my heart out when I wrote this, howled my emotions onto the page," he said. "I've been through a lot, made plenty of enemies in the UQ Police Department. I took quite a risk just publishing that." He handed the second copy of his book to me. "I brought a spare for you, Shamble."

Alvina flipped to the title page. "Is it autographed?"

Hairy Harry extended a black claw and tore a scratch through his name. "There you go, kid. Personalized."

With a sinking feeling, I realized that he expected us to read the book right there. I handed the copy to Robin, and she said, "We'll give it due consideration, sir. We look forward to reading it when we have time."

The rogue cop grumbled, "Everything's there—the corruption I exposed, the gang leaders I took down, the politicians whose throats I ripped out." Looking at Alvina, he seemed embarrassed. "Might want to skip chapter eight, girl. It gets a little steamy when I spill my guts about the brief, torrid relationship I had with that sexy vampire coroner."

Alvina flipped immediately to chapter eight and began reading.

Robin handed the spare copy back to me. "So long as you didn't violate any nondisclosure agreements, Mr. Harry, your story is your own to tell."

He took the book from my hands. "I want my story read! I talk about my rough patches. The climax is the terrible day in that shadowy warehouse, when everything fell apart." He closed his big, glowing eyes and lowered his head.

I remembered his rookie partner who'd been killed in the incident. "Amy Littlemiss."

He gnashed his fangs. "Little Amy Littlemiss! So eager and so innocent. Nothing's been the same since that day. I still blame myself."

Hairy Harry and his partner had found the distribution hub for a counterfeit Hummel figurine operation run by a mummy mobster named Lenny Linens. Hairy Harry and his rookie partner had split up in the warehouse, hunting among the crates of fake monster figurines. The werewolf cop was keyed up, wanting to get the bad guys with extreme prejudice (though he would have bitten the head off of anyone who accused him of being prejudiced). Lenny Linens shot at him, and Hairy Harry blasted back with his .44 magnum silver bullets.

Right through a crate of cute vampire shepherd-boy figurines.

And Amy Littlemiss had been on the other side.

"It's all in there." The werewolf scratched the glossy front of the cover. "All my angst, my guilt." Suddenly self-conscious, he glanced at his watch. "Uh, I need to get back soon to feed Lucky and take him on a walk." He drew a deep breath, a rattling, threatening sound, and looked at Alvina. "I got my hellhound as a service dog to help with my PTSD. I love Lucky."

"I can't wait to meet your doggie," she said. "Is he friendly?"

"Not supposed to be." Hairy sounded disappointed. "He's made all the difference in my life." He looked at the book again. "And so has writing this memoir, just by getting it off my chest. My story could help others who find themselves in the same situation, and it could also warn unwitting collectors from buying unofficial monster Hummel figurines."

"That is a persistent problem," Robin said.

Sheyenne drifted forward. "But how can we help you, sir? Why did you need to see Alvina?"

He looked down at the copy of *Make My Day*. "I self-published the book because I needed to get it out there. Didn't waste time on any editing or formatting, because it's more *raw* this way. But it hasn't gotten much traction in the marketplace, and I'm still hoping to sell at least ten copies. Girl, with your blog readers on *I Was a Teenage Vampire*, and your Monstagram and your Sick-Tok followers, and ... well, because you're *cute*, maybe you could help me add some hashtags or whatever. Make me trendy."

"Trending," Alvina corrected. She flipped through the book, paused again on chapter eight. I gently removed the copy from her hands. She considered. "I can mention it in my blog, maybe interview you, take some pictures for Monstagram. Let me develop a social-media outreach plan."

Hairy Harry scratched the gray fur on his muzzle. "Can't thank you enough, girl." Then he turned to me and Robin. "With those Shamble & Die mysteries, you must have a connection with a good publisher. Could you talk to the editor about this project? It's sure to be a bestseller, or at least a ..." He paused to add with slow import, "Or a *beast* seller! Har! I thought that up myself. We can use it on the front cover, but I'd have to change to a different font so it stands out."

I didn't tell him that I was planning on a trip to Howard Phillips Publishing that afternoon. "We'll see what we can do, sir."

"Meanwhile I'll start figuring out what I need to get you more exposure," Alvina said. "I can come up with a list of bullet points. Silver bullet points!"

She giggled at her own joke, and Hairy Harry guffawed.

"We may need to paint another line on the office door, Beaux," Sheyenne said to me. "Include Alvina as a social-media consultant."

"Consulting is a vague and indefinable term," I said, remembering our basement neighbor, G. Latinous.

Full of energy, Hairy Harry bounded toward the door. "Got to get back to Lucky now. I miss my baby puppy." He glanced over his shoulder as he yanked the door open. "Thank you, girl. You're going to be a big help."

CHAPTER 17

When Sheyenne, Alvina, and I went to Howard Phillips Publishing that afternoon, I wasn't sure how to bring up Hairy Harry's self-published memoir. A good strategy might be to hide the cover and hope for the best.

The lobby bookstore had a clearance table set up with "Special Half Off" on the Shamble & Die adventures that Robin and I had signed at the *Necronomicon* gala. Maybe it would get a few more readers.

Alvina pushed all the elevator buttons, insisting that it was expected of her. The lurching stop and start of the elevator car reminded me of a half-asleep zombie trying to navigate an obstacle course.

The publishing offices on the thirteenth floor had been restored to normal business, with ringing phones, production staff in cubicles, busy editors staring at monitor screens. Book announcement posters focused on the special 12 + 1 anniversary edition of the *Necronomicon*.

Bolted to the floor in the main reception area was the display pedestal holding the original bloodstained tome. Sensor wires were ready to set off silent, or very noisy, alarms if anyone disturbed the collector's item. The air around the case held a haze of ozone and crackling magic.

I tipped my fedora to the receptionist, then we headed back to where Mavis and Alma Wannovich shared a corner office. Since a caricature of my face appeared on the Shamble & Die covers, many of the workers recognized me. When someone asked for my autograph, I pointed out that there were signed copies down in the lobby bookstore.

In the corner office, Alma left her plastic blow-up wallowing pool and waddled toward us. Sheyenne and the little girl greeted her, while avoiding splatters of the mud slurry. At her desk Mavis finished typing an email and smiled up at us.

I reported, "Robin and I went to check on Stella Artois yesterday. She's fine, and when I reminded her about the signature pages, she said to send them over."

"Wonderful! Such a chore. Not everyone is so reliable, Mr. Shamble."

"Librarians usually are," Sheyenne said.

"But *celebrity* librarians might be a different matter." Mavis scratched the wart on the side of her hooked nose and picked up the phone. She punched in an extension and said in a syrupy voice, "This is Mavis. Is Howard or Philip in? We have a special guest." She nodded, then hung up. "Wait here a moment, Mr. Shamble. Philip would like to see you."

Alvina poked among the stacked manuscripts on Mavis's desk, then looked at another pile beside the wallowing pool. The big sow waddled back to the muddy water and settled in for more reading.

"Any special titles coming up that we should look forward to?" Sheyenne asked. "Other than the *Necronomicon* anniversary edition?"

Mavis flipped through a folder. "We're updating the perennially popular cookbook *To Serve Man* to make it more gender neutral."

Philip Phillips arrived, looking dapper in a charcoal-gray three-piece suit. "Mr. Chambeaux, thank you for your efforts with Stella Artois. The special autograph pages are ready— would you be so kind as to deliver them to her? I believe she trusts you."

"She let us into her house, but I don't know if that means she trusts me."

"It means exactly that," said Philip. "The receptionist up front will have the signature sheets. Thank you very much for doing this favor."

I considered, then reconsidered, and considered again, then finally brought up Hairy Harry's book. At least I could tell him I'd tried. "Perhaps you could do us a favor, Mr. Phillips. One of our clients, a well-known rogue werewolf cop, has written a very candid memoir about the poor decisions in his life. The book was previously self-published, but he's seeking wider distribution."

Alma splashed in the slurry of brown water, and Mavis sat up. "Hairy Harry? Hmmm, could be interesting."

Philip looked embarrassed. "Howard Phillips Publishing is a reputable company. We aren't looking for scandalous celebrity tell-all books."

"But it's really good," Alvina said. "Especially chapter eight."

Philip searched for a graceful way to decline the submission. "I'm afraid we don't take unagented manuscripts."

Alvina brightened. "I'm his agent."

The publisher kept retreating from the office. "Send it to Alma and Mavis. They'll consider it carefully and give you an objective rejection." Insisting on pressing business, he wove his way through the labyrinth of cubicles to the vaults of his executive offices.

I left the manuscript with Mavis and headed back out to the reception desk, where we picked up the package waiting for us, a thick stack the size of two reams of paper.

The elevator bell dinged, and Linda Bullwer emerged. The frumpy vampire woman pushed the cat's-eye glasses up on her nose as she noticed us. "Mr. Shamble, did you come to see me? I don't have offices in the building. I work remotely."

"We're here on other business." I hefted the stack of signature sheets. "Do you need to interview me about our current cases? You must be working on the next novel."

"I have a much bigger deadline." She lowered her voice. "And a higher advance."

"What is it?" Alvina asked.

"A secret project."

"Can you tell me the secret?" The girl held up her little finger. "Pinky swear not to tell."

Linda reached out with her own little finger to hook it into the vampire girl's. "Well, we are in the publishing offices … and it'll be announced soon. I'm very excited!" She could barely contain her energy, as if she had just consumed a triple-strength caffeinated blood drink.

The ghostwriter leaned closer. "My name won't go on the cover, but the project will make literary history." She lowered her voice even further. "I'm writing a sequel—an authorized sequel."

"Sequel to what?" I asked.

"The timing is perfect and the market will be huge. I'm doing a sequel to the *Necronomicon*! Once everybody reads the new special edition, they'll want to know what happens next. My sequel will have more action, unexpected plot twists, and new characters you'll love to hate. Imitating the style is going to be the hardest part, but I'm up to the challenge. They hired the right ghostwriter."

"Congratulations," I said, though I wasn't so sure about the idea.

"I hope it doesn't suck," Alvina said. "Sequels are never as good as the original."

CHAPTER 18

Returning to the offices, Alvina was overjoyed with the stack of free sample books the receptionist had given her, although Sheyenne wasn't convinced they were appropriate for a little girl, vampire or otherwise.

Alvina darted ahead of us into the building and dodged around the large blob who was laboriously making his way down the main hallway to the basement stairs. Being incorporeal, Sheyenne wafted through him and didn't need to dodge anything at all as she went up the stairs.

I paused inside the door to give G. Latinous slurching room along the stained carpeting.

"Excuse me," he said. "Coming through. Sorry to be a bother."

"I'm not in a hurry," I replied.

"I was just turning in some paperwork to the building super." The blob reached the top of the basement stairs, bunched up his body, and heaved the front end over the lip. Gravity took hold of his amorphous form and pulled him down like a Slinky made of snot. G. glooped down one stair at a time to the basement with a sound like a bucket of phlegm being poured down a drain.

Renfeld shuffled out on his ponderous rounds. He wore a grin or a grimace (hard to tell with damaged lips and broken teeth). I gave him a polite wave, then started up the stairs to avoid a conversation, but Renfeld increased his pace to meet me.

Right at the top of the basement stairs, though, he slipped on the fresh ooze. His feet flew out from under him, and he tumbled down to the basement. The inarticulate grunts of alarm ended with a squish, and I feared he had split his skull open and spilled brains everywhere.

I hurried after him, careful to avoid the deepest slime. "Mr. Renfeld, are you all right?"

Miraculously, the ghoul's landing had been cushioned by the blob consultant. Arms and legs akimbo, Renfeld struggled to extract himself from the mass.

G. adjusted his bulk and ejected Renfeld. "Sorry, sorry! I always seem to be in the way." The ghoul brushed himself off and tried to recover his pride, though he hadn't had much pride in the first place.

As I helped him up, Renfeld tugged on his rumpled shirt, wiggled a loose tooth. "How do I look, Mr. Shamble?"

His blotched and leprous skin ranged from gray to sickly green. I looked at his hollow, bruised-looking cheeks, the shadows around his eyes, the spiky clumps of unwashed hair. "You look just fine."

He let out a watery sigh of relief. "The stairs are hazardous, but it would be awkward if I had to sue the building super for lack of maintenance."

After G. Latinous moved down the hall to his unit, I offered to help Renfeld back up the stairs, but he decided just to do his rounds in the lower level. So, I made my way back to the second floor, hoping for a less dramatic afternoon.

Alvina sat at her table with the stack of freebie books, as well as one of Hairy Harry's copies of *Make My Day*. She was busy taking notes. At first I assumed she was doing homework, but then I saw her making a list of marketing ideas. She smiled at me. "Since I'm representing Mr. Harry as his agent, I want to present an organized social-media plan. I bet he can get a good book deal."

I chuckled. "What do you know about book deals, kid?"

"I'm an *agent*." She let out an exasperated sigh. "I don't have to know anything."

The kid was already more familiar with the publishing industry than I was.

Sheyenne had the office TV on with the sound turned down, playing a talking-heads commentary program. The disembodied head in question was a familiar pundit whose name was listed as simply "Dick," with no last name. Dick the Head was hosting a retrospective on thirteen years of the Big Uneasy.

He was certainly a familiar face to us. Robin had represented Dick in one of her first landmark unnatural cases, not long after he had become significantly shorter.

Preoccupied, Robin stepped out of her office with her yellow legal pad and a stack of manila folders. "Interesting new case, Dan. Involves a zombie organ donor. Legal and ethical issues."

"Any detective work involved?" I asked.

"Maybe some lost and found. When the plaintiff died, his lungs, liver, and kidneys were removed and transplanted into organ recipients. But now he's returned as a zombie and wants the pieces back. His organ-donor card had a lot of gray areas."

I frowned. "Does he actually need to use them anymore?"

"Not relevant to the claim of ownership," she replied. "But the organ recipients are certainly using them, and they claim they did not enter into the arrangement expecting it to be a non-permanent lease." She sighed. "It'll probably be another case with no legal precedent, and I'll be in the news again."

On TV, Dick the Head was saying, "Those first years were rough. As if it wasn't difficult enough for me adjusting to being a zombie—and not in very good condition, I might add—I had to deal with the sheer hate and inhumanity. Inhumanity among humans! That really made my heart sink."

Dick's brow furrowed in deep concentration. He was trying to shake his head, but was no longer connected to any shoulders.

Watching the TV, Robin pressed her lips together in a hard frown. "Such a sad case—one of the main reasons I decided to devote my life to helping unnaturals get justice. What happened to him was so shocking."

Dick was an innocuous zombie, minding his own business, and became the first recorded case of a zombie lynching. A group of rowdy good ol' boys decided to have some fun with the slow-moving shambler. They tied poor Dick to two beat-up pickup trucks and pulled him apart by driving in different directions. The head popped right off.

Being a zombie, Dick's head was still articulate enough to name his attackers and describe in slurred but graphic detail what they had done to him. The incident got a great deal of media attention. Even normally sour and hard-hearted commentators admitted that Dick had been badly mistreated.

Young firebrand lawyer Robin Deyer took the case, even made Dick testify. The decapitated head pulled on heartstrings as he told his chilling story. Dick the Head won his case. The good-ol'-boy lynchers went to jail for a well-deserved life sentence, and Dick became famous for his mournful plea. "Can't we all just get along?"

Afterward, Robin went on her crusade, insisting that

monsters were people, too. She turned the legal system upside down, forcing major reforms that had never been considered before. I admired her for it, never dreaming that we'd eventually become business partners.

Robin listened to Dick now as he reminisced about those early days on TV. "After all that, I'm so glad he managed to get ahead. He just got his own daily show on WRIP."

Chapter 19

While I reviewed the footage from Elm Street's neighborhood-watch security cameras, Sheyenne was doing battle with the mold monster again in our kitchenette. I could hear the frustration in her voice as she retorted, "Don't you use that language on me!"

Originally, she had spotted a blurry black smudge growing on the wall beside the refrigerator, and their relationship had progressively deteriorated for the past month. The smear of black mold seemed innocuous enough at first—until it fought back.

Mold was not an uncommon problem in the damp and dreary Unnatural Quarter, and Sheyenne didn't think twice when she sprayed the mold with a common corrosive household cleaner. When the substance bubbled and drooled, she had wiped it away, leaving the wall nice and clean. No more mold.

Within days, the mold reappeared in a darker, more aggressive pattern, which she scoured again and added stronger bleach. The third time, the foul black tendrils curled along the wall, looping and forming lines. The mold spelled out the words *LEAVE ME ALONE!*

So, the aggressive mold was not just a domestic cleaning problem, but a sentient substance. Robin claimed that another dose of kitchen cleaner would violate the mold's rights. In a mediation attempt, she started contacting local contractors to see if they could cut out the fungally inhabited drywall and replace it with uncontaminated sheetrock.

When she informed Renfeld that we intended to replace that section of wall, though, he forwarded the request to the building management company. Within days, we received a firm denial, stating that such modifications to the unit were not covered in our lease agreement.

I wondered if the mold had blackmailed the managers.

When Alvina began coughing from an allergic reaction, though, Sheyenne and I had had enough, and even Robin put her legal concerns aside. Sheyenne scrubbed the mold clean and added a third dose of potent mold-destroyers, but the following day, the mold had returned with a vengeance, spelling out in capital letters, *I'LL KILL YOU FOR THIS, BITCH!*

Then it was all-out war.

After Robin took photos of the clear threat made by the aggressive spores, Sheyenne resorted to using a scrub brush and a solvent so potent the toxic fumes made even her spectral form shimmer and blur.

Thus, for that reason, Sheyenne wasn't at the reception desk when the phone rang, so I answered in my best professional voice. A gruff snarl came back at me. "Shamble, is that you? This is Hairy Harry."

"Hello, Mr. Harry." Across the room, Alvina perked up from her homework. "Hold on a sec. You'll be impressed with everything Alvina's done since we last—"

"Shut up, punk! I don't need the vampire girl. Well ... I do, but not this instant. I'll look over her marketing strategy when the whole damn world isn't falling apart. I need *you*, Shamble! You've got to help me. I'm not safe."

With my free hand I snagged my fedora and jacket from the wall hook. "On my way." My .38 hung in its holster on the hat rack, out of reach. "Is it a shoot-out? Should I call for backup?"

"You're my backup, punk! Something's wrong. Seriously wrong!" He howled in frustration.

I heard a louder barking and snarling in the background. "Is that Lucky? Is he okay?"

"Lucky and I are fine, but we're the only ones. I just took him out on a walk around the Quarter. I let him eat pigeons and chase pedestrians. That's how he gets his exercise."

"Then what's the problem?"

Alvina approached with her laptop and her notes. The werewolf's voice was so loud, the whole office could hear him. "Lucky and I got back home, and my whole neighborhood's gone! Stripped of every living thing, like all the people evacuated."

"Evacuated?" These days it wasn't out of the question that some lava sprite might trigger a volcanic eruption, or a storm goblin could summon a cyclone or two. "We haven't received any notice of imminent natural disasters. Why would your neighborhood be evacuated?"

"I got no notice!" Hairy Harry snarled. "If there was a disaster evacuation, then I should have been invited, too."

Lucky continued to yowl in the background. I had to hold the phone away from my ear. A chill went through my embalming fluid. This sounded just like what had happened with Mary Celeste's neighborhood.

"And I don't see any disasters coming, Shamble," the werewolf continued. "It's just peaceful—and that makes me nervous."

"I'll be right over," I said. "This may well tie in to another missing neighborhood case I'm working."

Alvina was eager to follow me, but I shook my head. "Not today, kid. You've got schoolwork."

My detective instincts were on high alert. One vanishing neighborhood was a mystery.

Two vanishing neighborhoods was a pattern.

That's what we were taught in P.I. school, though the unit on vanishing neighborhoods had been lacking in detail and pragmatic advice. I hoped Mary was still safely ensconced at the Motel Six Feet Under, at least when she wasn't washing dishes at the Ghoul's Diner.

I'D BEEN TO HAIRY HARRY'S HOME DURING THE DOGNAPPING case. The ranch-style home had brick walls and aluminum awnings over the windows. The sidewalk and cement driveway showed plenty of cracks. The backyard was a dog run enclosed with a chain link fence topped with barbed wire. An iron stake and chain in the patchy lawn marked where the hellhound spent the days outside. A folding lawn chair sat on the porch, where Hairy Harry could watch his pet growl at trespassers.

Seeing me turn the corner, the werewolf bounded down the empty street with his pony-sized hound on a leash. Lucky bared his tusk-like fangs and let out a loud yelp that made me cringe. The hellhound lunged on his leash, and Hairy Harry bunched his muscles, using all his strength to hold the animal back. The spiked collar bit into the puppy's throat. Lucky seemed to think it was just play, and his tail wagged back and forth like a cudgel.

Hairy Harry jerked the leash again and shoved the hound's hindquarters down. "Sit! Sit! Good doggie."

"Hi, Lucky. Remember me?" The hellhound whined. I bent down, and the enormous beast licked the side of my face with an abrasive tongue the size of a beach towel. Normally, hellhound slobber has a high acidic content that could eat through floors, but Lucky had been on a special diet.

The werewolf looked around, agitated. "Last time I needed your help, Shamble, it was because Lucky disappeared. Now the pup's here—but everything else is gone!" He gestured down the street. "Too damn quiet. Something smells funny."

I inhaled deeply, but I detected only the hellhound's fur and Hairy Harry's muskier scent.

I saw mailboxes, modest homes, a few with swing sets, a few with gallows. Nothing stirred. The windows weren't shuttered, curtains and shades not drawn. It was just a normal day. People should have been going about their business—except there were no people in sight.

"This is a matter for the police, Mr. Harry. Why didn't you call the cops?"

He worked his muzzle and spat in disgust. "Cops! I know the corruption on the force. They're all out to get me. Maybe the UQPD erased my neighborhood just to scare me. All the embarrassing things in my memoir are going to blow the lid off the whole department … if anybody reads it."

He yanked on Lucky's leash, and the hellhound bounded back toward the house. The werewolf cop staggered after him. "Follow me, Shamble—got something for you. It needs to be in your custody, in case something happens to me."

He hooked the hellhound's leash to the iron stake in the yard and opened the front door, but didn't invite me inside. I waited on the driveway, looking at the house, while the hellhound looked at me, scarlet eyes blazing, tongue hanging out. His wagging tail battered the lawn.

Hairy Harry returned with a thick manuscript in his paws. "New version of the book, extra chapters—even more controversial than the first draft."

I reluctantly took the stack of paper. "Not sure I should have this, sir."

"It's important! And you're the only one I trust!" His bushy eyebrows raised up, and his expression became hopeful. "Maybe you could get it to the publisher? You said an editor might be willing to have a look."

"Anything for a client," I said.

He unhooked the leash and whistled to his hellhound. Full of energy, Lucky bounded into the house, and I could hear furniture crashing, shelves tumbling.

The werewolf cop turned back at me, suspicious. "I've got to stay here and keep myself safe." He retreated through the front door and slammed it in my face. I heard a succession of deadbolts and chains being set.

I stayed long enough to inspect the street. It was indeed empty, the residents evacuated, or teleported, or just gone. Not a neighbor was stirring, not even a giant mutated lab rat.

As I headed away, pondering the mystery, I ran into a man in old-fashioned garb, a felt hat cocked on his head, pocketwatch connected to a silk vest under a dark jacket with tails. Clearly another Olde Tymer, though not one of those who had disrupted the *Necronomicon* gala. I gave him a hard, suspicious look, but the man just kept gazing into the quiet empty street.

Earlier that day, I had done more research into the Olde Tymers. They were a known extremist conspiracy organization, though they seemed to be all talk and no action, likely due to disorganization rather than lack of any malicious intent. At various times, the Olde Tymers had claimed that the Big Uneasy wasn't real, that the magic had never occurred, that no monsters had reappeared in the world. Despite all the obvious evidence, they insisted that unnaturals were a hoax perpetrated by the corrupt media.

One particular inflammatory post said that the restored monsters were an attempt to flood the polls with unregistered monsters to overturn the next election, although no one could say which political party monsters might vote for. Often, the Olde Tymers turned their anger against poor Stella Artois, blaming her for everything.

This man, however, was by himself as he gazed like a tourist into the uncomfortably empty neighborhood. Suspecting he was up to no good, I approached. "Can I help you, sir?"

The man ran his eyes up and down my zombie appearance as if I were little better than gum stuck to the bottom of his shoe. Looking at the empty sidewalks and silent houses, he mused, "No, I'm just here enjoying the view. Just like the good old days ... not a monster in sight."

CHAPTER 20

s I always say, the cases don't solve themselves. Sheyenne reminds me, though, that errands don't run themselves either. And I had a full list for today.

For my caseload, I needed to understand what had happened to Hairy Harry's missing neighborhood, which meant I'd better check on Mary Celeste as well. Maybe I could compare the two empty streets.

The Elm Street neighborhood-watch cameras had shown nothing. For budgetary reasons, the cameras took only one image per day, and the recordings had not provided any evidence. So I wanted to look for other clues.

And I needed to check on our car at Wrex's Auto Repair, since they still hadn't given us an estimate, and the gremlin did not answer his phone.

Robin also reminded me about delivering the thousand signature sheets for Stella to sign.

It was going to be a busy day.

After dropping off Hairy Harry's salacious manuscript at the office, I grabbed the keys to our loaner hearse. The big vehicle was never going to replace our beloved Pro Bono Mobile, but it was a nice ride (better in the front seat than the back). The signature sheets made a big enough stack in the passenger seat that I buckled them in for safety.

Before I eased the dark vehicle into the streets of the Quarter, I let a pair of squid monsters pedal by on a two-seated bicycle, moving with a flurry of slippery appendages. Then I headed toward the industrial district with its junkyards and mechanical graveyards—including Wrex's Auto Repair. First things first.

I parked next to a pair of squashed Volkswagen Beetles. I didn't see the Pro Bono Mobile on the front lot or among the automobile skeletons in the back. Robin's lime-green Ford Maverick was butt ugly, and the rust patches only made the color scheme more distinctive, but at least I could spot it anywhere. I hoped the car was in the repair bay.

A polite bell jingled as I entered Wrex's front office, but no one could hear with the racket of the repair bay—loud power drills, hydraulic lifts, blasts of air pressure, and giggling gremlins. Wrex sat on his spinning stool next to the bowl of randomly arranged keys, pecking away at his desktop computer. He looked up at me. "Oh, you're the one with the hearse. Fine vehicle, isn't it?"

"It is, but it's not mine. Do you have an estimate on our own car? How close are the repairs?"

"Winkin, Blinkin, and Todd did a full diagnostic. It's almost finished. Repairs are guaranteed."

"Good to hear." I glanced past the boss into the repair bay. "Can I have a look?"

A stripped-down World War II army tank was up on the hydraulic lift, and one of the gremlins—Blinkin, I think—was chiseling out mud between the treads. The other two bays were empty.

I frowned. "Ours is the lime-green Maverick. I don't see it."

A gremlin mechanic swung from the ceiling chain, whooping it up. He let go of the hook and flew into a tall stack of metal shelves laden with auto parts. An avalanche of air filters toppled over and bounced along the floor.

"Lime green?" Wrex looked down at his monitor, typed in my name. "Oh, sorry, I had it listed as rust-colored. Winkin and Blinkin are nearly finished with the tune-up. Pretty soon it'll purr like a sleeping dragon." He cackled. "And it'll roar to life when you need it."

"I just need it for transportation." I stepped around the counter to get a better view of the repair bays. "Are you sure it's in there? That car is hard to miss."

Wrex hurried after me. "Hey, you can't go back there alone. Safety concerns."

"I'm already dead." I pushed open the door.

I looked at the bins of broken axles, hubcaps, even a large collection of seat belt buckles. One coffee can was filled with lug nuts; another held cigarette lighters.

"Those are just spare parts," Wrex explained. "We'll install anything you need."

"I need my vehicle. The entire vehicle."

"Of course you do! Owning a car, the American Dream." The gremlin smiled, showing his pointy teeth. "We'll help you meet your dreams."

"My dream is to have our own vehicle back. Where is it?" Wrex was being evasive, which triggered my detective instincts. I looked along the shelves, saw more headlights, a car battery, an oil filter, and jugs of colorful windshield-washer fluid and antifreeze, like the top-shelf selection in a fancy bar.

A flash of lime green caught my attention, and I stalked over to the shelves to find a front tire panel and a hood—definitely from the Pro Bono Mobile! I would have recognized the dents and rust anywhere. Behind a stack of spare tires was one of the Maverick's doors.

"That's my car! It's not finished—there's hardly anything left of it!"

"Oh, it's all there. We're just doing a tune-up," Wrex insisted. "We keep finding little things that need tinkering, because we take pride in our work. Some assembly required. You can trust us."

On the high shelf above, I spotted a familiar taillight. "Where's our vehicle?"

"We're rebuilding it from the bottom up. Good as new, I promise! Even better. It's all covered in your premier plan." He lowered his voice, sounding conciliatory. "You do have the nice loaner vehicle, after all. We'll get right on it, you'll see!"

I was heartsick to see the condition of the faithful Pro Bono Mobile, but there was nothing I could do. At this stage, I hoped the gremlins had installed all their defects and disrepairs and would start turning it around soon. Wrex would not want Robin Deyer to slip into lawsuit mode.

"Call us with an update," I growled. "And don't take too long!"

Suspended on the hydraulic lift, the military tank swiveled its turret, aimed the long cannon at me, then swung back. Winkin was just teasing.

Unsettled, I drove the hearse away from Wrex's Auto Repair. I wouldn't give Robin or Sheyenne a full report, not yet.

For my next stop I headed for the librarian's gated community, so I could hand-deliver the signature sheets. Donald the zombie guard still sat listless in his security shack, just watching the traffic go by. When I pulled up, he didn't remember me, nor did he find me listed on the clipboard, so I wrote my name on the bottom again, which satisfied him.

When the heavy gate lifted, I drove the hearse over the lowered drawbridge above the shark-and-crocodile-infested moat.

Stella Artois's house looked as quaint and charming as before, but this time I didn't have Robin's reassuring presence. The barbed wire, the KEEP OUT and NO TRESPASSING signs, and the lumpy lawn minefield put me in a cautious mood. I carried the signature sheets under my arm as I walked up to the front door.

I couldn't blame Stella for wanting to be left alone so she could read books and build her miniature models. On the other hand, such protective measures seemed extreme. Despite the importance of these signature sheets, I didn't want to be blown to bits delivering them.

Sheyenne had tried to call the librarian to let her know I was coming—and to request that the security systems be deactivated—but no one answered. I crept cautiously up the porch steps, still concerned about a trapdoor under the welcome mat.

I rang the doorbell and waited, and waited, then rang it again. Maybe Stella was assembling a new model in her secret, locked craft room. Where else would a recluse go?

Shifting the heavy wrapped sheets under my right arm, I peered into the front window, then went to the other side and squinted through a gap in the curtains. The house was quiet, dark, and empty. Stella did not seem to be home.

I considered walking around back, but decided against it, given the ominous defenses and danger signs. I didn't want to leave the valuable package on the empty porch.

Well, I had other errands to run. Howard Phillips Publishing could wait for their signature sheets.

CHAPTER 21

Zombies are known for being persistent and relentless, but I prefer to say "thorough." I kept considering where I might look for the reclusive librarian if she wasn't at home, but I moved on to the other items on my To Do list.

As I drove out through the imposing gate, I gave a brisk wave to Donald, but the guard zombie was so slow to respond that I barely caught him raising his hand in the hearse's rearview mirror.

Next on my list of errands, I went to revisit Mary Celeste's Elm Street, now that I had also seen Hairy Harry's empty neighborhood. There must be some connection. For a zombie detective, the proper term is "reconnoitering," and a good reconnoiter can provide a solution, or at least a good twist, to any case.

When I got to Elm Street, though, I found another big surprise. Instead of being a ghost town without ghosts, now Mary's neighborhood was busy, bustling, and terrifyingly *normal*.

Leaving the hearse parked on the street, I stared at mother monsters watching their children monsters play on the side-walk. An Igor-based lawn service worked on two different front yards, pushing loud mowers. A mummy was hanging clean linens to drip dry on a clothesline.

An old vampire in a bathrobe sat in the deep shade of a maple tree. A lizard demon sprayed a garden hose, washing his car in the driveway. A zombie in a tattered gray business suit bent down with excruciating slowness to pick up the news-paper at the end of the drive.

It was horrifying.

I studied the streetlight and stop sign on the corner, searching for hidden teleportation machinery, but Elm Street was just Elm Street—an everyday slice of the Unnatural Quarter painted by Norman Rockwell after a particularly bizarre fever dream.

I walked slowly past the mundane homes. A little werewolf kid bicycled up to me, gripping the handlebars with his paws to keep his balance, although the training wheels kept him upright. He pedaled by and rang his bell.

Two doors down, a teenage werewolf, possibly his older brother, held a baseball glove and tossed a softball back and forth with his dad. Seeing me, the teen wolf tossed the ball at me. "Here, mister—catch!"

I reached up, fumbled, and by some miracle managed to catch the softball. I lobbed it back. "Have you all lived here long?"

"About ten years," said the werewolf dad, catching the ball as his son tossed it again, and he flung it back with a flick of the furry wrist. The werewolf teen lunged with predatory speed and caught the ball in his glove.

"How about two days ago?" I asked. "Anything unusual happen?"

"Well …" The werewolf dad grumbled deep in his throat as he considered. "Connie made meatloaf when it was spaghetti night, and that sparked quite an animated dinner-table discus-sion. Other than that …" He turned toward his teen son, who kept slapping the baseball into his glove. "Anything you remember, Chad?"

"Nope," said the young werewolf. "Mr. Hamilton's little poodle got eaten by one of Miss Gardenia's Venus flytraps in the flowerbed, but we pried him out before he was digested too much."

I was alarmed. "Is it all right?"

"The dog or the Venus flytrap?" asked the werewolf dad.

"They're both fine," Chad answered. "I even fed the Venus flytrap some of Mom's meatloaf, and it seemed happy enough." The father glared at him, but Chad just shrugged. "It was supposed to be spaghetti night! Didn't taste right."

The little furball werewolf pedaled by on the sidewalk, ringing his bell.

I reached the next driveway by the time the zombie in the business suit had managed to pick up the newspaper. Maybe he would be more helpful. The name on the mailbox said "K. Hamilton." I realized he must be the owner of the partially digested poodle.

"Excuse me, I'm Dan Chambeaux, private detective." Then I added with emphasis, "*Zombie* detective."

He gave me a brotherly smile. "I'm Kris Hamilton. With a K." He paused, then clarified. "In the Kris part, not the Hamilton part."

"Are you familiar with this neighborhood, sir?"

"Always here."

That was a relief. "And where were you two days ago?"

The confusion was plain on Hamilton's face as he worked his mind through the question. "Two days? What do you mean?"

"This whole neighborhood disappeared. I came to investigate after we received complaints." I gestured up and down the street. "Every house here was empty. All the bikes abandoned. Not a person in sight."

Mr. Hamilton held his mail and his newspaper as he thought long and hard. "Oh. We were all on errands."

"Errands? All of you at the same time? Every single household?"

"Important errands. We're all back now. Everything normal." Hamilton's lips stretched in a smile. "Home sweet home."

"But I went from place to place. It was a ghost town."

"Ghosts." The zombie nodded slowly. "You'll want the Mohinders across the street." He pointed. "They're ghosts."

I would have noticed spectral presences flitting about when we searched the street. "They were gone, too."

Mr. Hamilton shrugged. "Everything's back to normal now. Perfect and happy."

Frustrated, I talked to some of the other residents—the lizard demon washing his car, the mummy hanging his laundry, even the Mohinder ghosts. But everyone insisted all was normal. Again and again, they gave me the same answer that the whole neighborhood had been out "on errands" two days ago.

They were returned home. Nothing to worry about.

Considering the previous cases I'd solved to great dramatic effect, the mystery of the missing neighborhood was a bit of a letdown. It wouldn't make for an exciting chapter in the next Shamble & Die novel.

Sometimes, you have to accept a win, that the cases really do solve themselves.

Leaving Elm Street, I returned to the Motel Six Feet Under so I could inform Mary that her neighborhood was back to nostalgically pleasant normal again. She could go home.

When I knocked on the door of her motel room, she came out wearing a white apron and rumpled multi-armed shirt, having just finished her shift at the diner. When the ambi-polydextrous young woman saw me, her face brightened, then fell, not sure whether I had good news or bad news.

When I told her that Elm Street was repopulated again, Mary asked me to take her home right away. Even with the motel's tempting amenities of color TV, air-conditioning, and lack of surveillance cameras, she just wanted to get back to her own townhouse.

She packed her things in a flurry while I checked out. At the front desk, vampire Shawna whisked the key out of my hand and stuffed it into a cubbyhole that held slithery, shadowy things. She punched my frequent-stay card. "Always happy to have your business, Mr. Shamble. We advertise witness-protection rates you know."

I carried Mary's bag to the hearse and tossed it into the spacious back cargo area. On the drive back to Elm Street, she was happy, said that things were looking up in her life. She was excited about an upcoming audition for a big hand-modeling job, then she vented about her hard hours at the Ghoul's Diner, the goo-encrusted dishes, the gnawed silverware, and worst of all—Esther, the harpy waitress.

I commiserated. I had dealt with Esther before.

We reached Elm Street and all of its strangely wholesome activity. I still had no explanation for what had happened. "Maybe it's like when you take an appliance in for repair, and it suddenly works just fine. Everything's normal now."

The werewolf furball bicycled by as we stood in front of her townhouse, ringing his bell. "Hi, Miss Celeste."

The mummy was taking down the dry brown linens from

the clothesline, and he waved a strip at her. "Welcome home, Miss Celeste."

The lizard demon was now waxing and buffing his car. He also gave a cheery wave.

Frustrated, Mary raised her voice. "Where were you all? You vanished!"

Mr. Hamilton shambled out of his garage. "No problem. Everything's back to normal."

"We were out on errands," said the werewolf dad.

Behind him, the furry mom popped open the front door, adjusting a flowery kitchen apron. "Yoo-hoo! It's spaghetti night tonight."

Mary's exasperation was rising. "They're too quiet, Mr. Shamble—too nice."

"That's not usually a reason to complain," I pointed out. I wondered if Hairy Harry's neighborhood would also restore itself.

The well-armed young woman shouldered her bag with a sigh. "I suppose you're right, Mr. Shamble. Do I need to go down to the police station and withdraw those missing-persons reports?"

"I'll send Officer McGoohan over. He loves to do paperwork."

Standing at her front door, Mary still seemed uneasy. I gazed down the pleasant street and tried to find it delightful. Something inside, though, told me not to call it Case Closed just yet.

CHAPTER 22

Leaving Elm Street, unsettled, I spotted something suspicious out of the corner of my eye.

Linda Bullwer lurked near a flowering dogwood bush, jotting down observations on her notepad. She was obviously trying to be unobtrusive, but achieved the opposite result.

I suspected she was following me.

Even with her big *Necronomicon* sequel project, Linda Bullwer was the type of hack writer—and I mean that in only a good way—who kept herself busy with multiple projects at a time. She came to our offices to pick up copies of case files (after Sheyenne blacked out any names for privacy). As the Shamble & Die series continued, Linda said she wanted to add greater depth to the characters, flesh out my morbid yet heart-warming personality, and insert more adjectives to convey the ambiance of the Unnatural Quarter.

As I cruised by in the hearse, the vampire ghostwriter ducked among the branches of the flowering dogwood, trying to stay out of sight. I couldn't understand why she would bother to hide from me.

Then, as the boughs and leaves grasped for her, I realized it was an ornamental species of carnivorous dogwood. And bloodsucking plants are not picky about their meals. Linda swatted at the thorny branches, making a scene, but they kept clawing at her. She thrashed about so much that she dropped her notepad.

I stopped the hearse and rushed over to rescue her. I grabbed her pale hand and pulled, but the canine branches fought back, scratching and nipping. It must have been a pit bull species of dogwood.

By the time I extricated Linda, her dress and sweater were frayed. The carnivorous tree continued to rattle its branches, and the red flowers twisted and growled.

"You should be more careful, Miss Bullwer." I gestured to a prominent warning sign at the base of the tree. *Beware of Dogwood.*

She had gone paler than usual. "I was taking important notes." She reached down just far enough to snatch her notepad from the ground. The branches snapped at her, but she managed to pull free without getting nipped. Embarrassed, she brushed down some of her loose hair and looked down at her pad. "Why were you on Elm Street, Mr. Shamble?"

"Working on a missing-persons case—multiple missing persons. Missing neighborhood, in fact. Weren't you here to observe me?"

"No, I was here on another matter entirely." She jotted down notes, then paused, indicating the mundane neighborhood. "The street looks normal to me."

"It was entirely empty two days ago, not a soul in sight. But everyone's back home now. It won't make for a very exciting chapter in a new Shamble & Die book. The case solved itself."

"I could always add a car chase," she mused. "Or some sex."

Still thinking of the mystery, I continued, "I've interviewed the formerly missing persons, and they're also missing any memory of what happened here."

"Exactly what I feared." Linda clicked her tongue against

her fangs. "Ever since the Big Uneasy, I've believed in more than my share of conspiracy theories. If all the neighbors vanished and then mysteriously returned, but they seem a little too normal and wholesome to be true ..." She lowered her voice. "Did you look inside the garage? Inside the houses? Under the beds?"

"What do you mean?"

Her face flushed with urgency. *"Did you check for pods?"*

"That, uh, didn't come up," I said.

She jotted down another note. "Maybe I should add that part to the novel? Put your character in peril, the whole world at risk of being taken over by mindless soul-sucking doppel-gangers?"

"You shouldn't stereotype, Miss Bullwer. I've met a doppel-ganger before, and they're not all mindless and soul-sucking."

Body snatchers and doppelgangers had been part of numerous conspiracy theories and wild explanations that arose after the Big Uneasy, since no one really knew what had caused it until much later. After the rules of magic and science changed, after supernatural creatures actually returned to the world, even the craziest conspiracy ideas became viable.

One popular story blamed a race of intelligent lizard people from the center of the earth, calling them powerbrokers who had caused the magical shift to happen. Others insisted that the Big Uneasy was the work of aliens, although it didn't make sense that aliens would bring back monsters. A mutant race of humans with psychic powers was also a possibility ... or Satanist covens and witchcraft craft circles. Ideas that would have been laughable at any other time were greeted with open minds.

Due to rampant suspicion, humans reacted badly to the ghosts, demons, and creatures that now walked the streets, mowed the lawns, and went out to restaurants. As with the case of Dick the Head, their response was to hunt down anything that looked like a monster, just because it was a monster.

Out of self-defense, unnaturals banded together to form militias so they could keep themselves safe. Many put aside ancient enmities, vampires and werewolves side by side defending their homes. Similarly, humans formed anti-monster militias, and it looked like an all-out war was brewing.

In one of Robin's early cases, a group of human hookers repeatedly beat up a vampire prostitute, even though vampires had a far longer tradition of being "ladies of the night." But the human hookers complained that the "fang-banger" was invading their territory, working their corner.

Using silver clubs and ash wood baseball bats, they pummeled, bruised, and smashed the vampire hooker, but when she went to the police station to file a complaint, her bruises and injuries had already healed. By the time the desk clerk got around to interviewing the vampire, she looked perfectly fine. When the vamp was beaten a second and third time, the police tried to document the injuries, but vampires don't show up on photographs either, which posed a different kind of problem.

When Robin pled her case, the human bully hookers received only a slap on the wrist, since there was no concrete evidence to submit. This injustice, after the Dick the Head case, enraged Robin and set her on her course in the Unnatural Quarter....

I remember the day when the news media finally reported the sensational explanation of the Big Uneasy, identifying the virgin librarian and her fateful paper cut. The alchemical experts and magical scholars turned Stella Artois into an instant celebrity.

Coincidentally, not long afterward, a race of intelligent lizard people did emerge from within the earth, where they were astounded to learn about all the conspiracy theories pinned on their peace-loving race. The lizard leader explained that his people had simply taken up the Amish faith and retreated to simpler times down in their caves, where they had access to only basic technology....

Now, coming out of my reverie, I looked over at Linda Bullwer. "I'll look for pods as I continue my investigation. But I think the Elm Street case is solved."

I only hoped that Hairy Harry's missing neighborhood would return just as easily. Since I still didn't know where to find Stella Artois to deliver the signature sheets, I headed back to the office. Most of my To Do list had been checked off.

Chapter 23

Traffic was a nightmare—and not the good sort of nightmare. The cars had slowed to a crawl near our office building, and since the loaner hearse took up a lane and a half, I parked on a side street and walked the rest of the way. Exercise helped keep me limber and well-preserved.

The reason for the jam soon became apparent. Some of the streets were closed off ahead, and cops directed traffic around a birthday/funeral/block party. A gargoyle Dixieland jazz band marched along, the members blowing on trumpets and trombones. A rock monster followed, using balled fists to pound on a big bass drum. A troll picked up the rear, tossing pawfuls of candy and clanking decorative iron chains.

The gargoyle trumpet player had the words *Happy Big Uneasy Day* painted on his outstretched wings, like a billboard. Even though several days had passed since the anniversary, schedules were hard to keep in the Quarter, and a late party was still a party.

I strolled along sidewalks crowded with parade watchers. A ghoul and a litch, obviously in love, sat on a blanket and shared a bottle of root beer.

"I hate clogs," said a burbling voice as a large rolling wad of slime joined me on the sidewalk.

I nodded a greeting to G. Latinous. "Trying to get back to the office, too?"

The blob shifted his form to raise a nodule that might have been a head. "Actually I'm out on errands—a shopping trip. I have a new client." He squished himself narrower as we came to a crowded patch between a fire hydrant and standing spectators.

"A shopping trip?" I was being polite, but also curious, since I was still not clear on the amorphous nature of the consulting profession.

"I procure things upon request. I find certain items and provide them to the client."

"Oh, like a home shopping assistant?"

His laugh sounded like a fart inside a witch's cauldron. "I have been hired by a famous librarian."

"Stella Artois? I know she doesn't like to go out in public. Are you buying groceries?"

"Oh, something much more special than that." He left a thick trail of mucous behind him like a garden slug fleeing from a saltshaker. "She's asked me to locate and buy a miniature train set, which she intends to build on her dining room table."

I nodded. "She does love her miniatures. Her collection is quite ambitious."

"You've seen it yourself then?" The blob seemed interested. "She allows very few visitors in the house."

"My partner and I went to see her on a matter for the publisher. Do you happen to know where she is today?" I raised the heavy stack of signature sheets under my arm. "I have an urgent package for her, but no one was home," I said, then added under my breath, "I hope she hasn't disappeared."

The blob paused. "Check the library. She doesn't leave the house often, but she enjoys going to the main branch incognito, remembering her old life as a librarian."

It was great to have a good lead—the best part of being a detective. "That's excellent information. Thank you."

After another half block, we turned away from the parade crowds onto a quiet side street. The gutters were recently swept, and someone had kindly laid out a welcome mat in front of a storm drain that led down into the sewers.

"This is where we part company, Mr. Shamble," G. Latinous said. He extended a pseudopod of snot into the gap, starting to pour himself into the drainage system.

"You're going to find a model train set down there?" I asked.

"There are numerous boutique shops. I've heard there's one called Underground Railroad." As he flowed into the storm drain, the remaining part of his oozing body formed into a new head lump. "Good luck finding Ms. Artois."

I hefted the signature sheets in acknowledgment as the blob finished going down the drain. Rather than getting back to the office, I headed for the UQ Public Library.

CHAPTER 24

The Unnatural Quarter public library main branch and vault of secrets was an imposing fortress of literacy, a thick-walled bastion of books where the fiction, nonfiction, and reference works were available only to those who dared.

No wonder the mousy librarian felt safe here.

The granite steps were wide and high, as if built for the stride of a Goliath rather than a women's reading club. Carrying the package of signature sheets, I ascended from the busy street toward the main pillared entrance, which was flanked by a pair of lion statues. The leonine figures looked majestic and wise, until they stirred, rose up on their massive paws, and curled back stone lips to expose stone teeth.

One statue raised a mammoth granite paw to stop me. "Show your library card."

I fumbled in my wallet, hoping I had it with me. "But I don't intend to check out any books."

"Then why come to the library?" growled the other statue.

"A social call."

"No talking allowed," said the lion.

"It's a quiet social call." I pulled out my private investigator's license, but that did not satisfy the giant feline guards. The statuary predators grew more incensed until finally I came upon the UQ library card. I flashed it in triumph as if it were a winning lottery ticket.

Both stone lions sat back on their haunches. "Good enough. Enjoy your visit."

In front of me, the doors opened and a nerdy-looking college student sauntered out wearing a backpack. Human students often visited the Quarter to study original source material when writing term papers on the social effects of the Big Uneasy.

One lion reached out with a paw and snagged his backpack, lifting him bodily into the air. "Not so fast! Got to make sure you're not smuggling any contraband."

As the panicked student's feet kicked and dangled in the air, the stone lions used their claws to unzip his backpack and rummage through the books. "Where's your receipt for these volumes you checked out?"

"Here, here!" He dug in his pockets and pulled out a printed slip of paper.

Depositing the student back on the steps, the stone lion nodded. "All right. Mind you don't turn them in late."

The other statue said, "You don't want to know about our overdue policy."

The flustered young man fled headlong down the stone stairs. While the twin statues were distracted, I hurried into the library.

Inside, the huge building had vaulted ceilings, dirty skylights, and a labyrinth of shelves. It was a mausoleum in which books were entombed. Dust motes drifted through watery sunbeams like weak spotlights illuminating the main gallery. Readers sat at long mahogany tables, others at carrels. A cyclops prowled through the cooking section, pressing his one eye close to the spines.

I had no idea where I might look for Stella Artois, especially if she was incognito. Though the very thought made my skin crawl, I knew what I'd have to do. I had no choice.

I needed to go to the reference desk.

On a previous case investigating a newt's missing eye, I had encountered Frieda the reference librarian, also known as the Spider Lady. I had not forgotten the experience.

I tiptoed forward, trying not to scuff the floor with my shoes. Frieda insisted on absolute quiet, which made it difficult to ask her questions.

The reference librarian sat in a tall chair, a woman whose face was as ageless as a prune from ancient Egypt. On a display board behind her high reference desk were numerous WANTED posters featuring patrons with overdue books.

Her gray hair had been pulled back and tied up in an excruciatingly tight bun, and her expression was like a tightly closed sphincter. Her stylish (in the 1950s) glasses held lenses thick enough to be used as astronomical instruments. Instead of counting sheep to fall asleep, she probably counted Dewey decimal numbers.

I lowered my voice to the barest of whispers. "Excuse me?"

Her eyes blazed red. "Keep your voice down! Other patrons are reading in peace." Her voice lashed through the library like a whip, and everyone else froze; some readers ducked under the tables.

As she stirred in the chair, her multiple limbs, which were previously hidden by the barrier of the desk, began to move. Attached to her torso were polished black spider legs, some ending in hooked claws, others in grasping pincers.

I couldn't back down, though. "I'm terribly sorry, but I need reference information, and only you can help me."

Mollified, she raised one jointed arachnid limb and pushed

the thick glasses up on her face. "Of course, sir. How may I help you?" Another leg snatched a request form from the stack on the counter. "Does it require an interlibrary loan?"

"I'm looking for someone who may be present in the library. A rather famous customer."

"The privacy of our patrons is paramount."

I raised the package of signature sheets. "I believe she'll want to see me. It's ..." I leaned over the desk and whispered, "It's *Stella Artois*, one of your fellow librarians."

"She was before my time," said Frieda, "but we do owe her a debt of gratitude for causing the Big Uneasy, unleashing countless unnaturals, and creating this fine library system." Another articulated limb tapped on the countertop. "She does indeed come here to read in peace. We've granted her access to the Cone of Silence."

"Could I talk with her?" I asked.

"If you talk with her, that defeats the purpose of the Cone of Silence."

"I promise I'll wait until she finishes a chapter."

The Spider Lady considered long and hard, then gave me directions, along with a warning that if she received any complaints whatsoever, my book-borrowing privileges would be revoked.

The Cone of Silence room reminded me of an NSA security vault for the inspection of classified documents. Looking through the narrow observation window in the door, I could see Stella sitting inside under bright fluorescent light, turning the pages of a novel.

I politely knocked, but she didn't flinch. I knocked harder, with the same result. I pounded and called out her name, but she still didn't notice me. The Cone of Silence worked perfectly.

I waited at the observation window, waving both hands. Finally, she glanced up while turning a page and caught the movement out of the corner of her eye. She slipped a leather bookmark with a yarn tassel into place and got up to let me inside. "Hello, Mr. Shamble. I didn't expect you to find me here."

"You weren't at home, and since I know you're still a librarian at heart ..."

When Stella closed the door, the silence returned like an empty bubble around us. Even my hushed voice seemed too loud. "The signature pages are ready for you to autograph," I said, holding up the heavy package. "It's a big stack."

She took the package and slipped it into a voluminous book bag on the floor beside the chair. "I agreed to do this, but I still cringe at the thought of ... writing in a book." Her voice carried enough disgust to make my hair curl.

"It's your autograph, ma'am. You're a celebrity," I said. "That's why people pay a premium for the special edition."

"People don't value the right things anymore." The librarian looked sad and disappointed. "Unnaturals celebrate me as a hero, but I wish the Big Uneasy had never happened. I long for my normal life. That's why I come here to read old books and remember happy, wholesome times."

She closed the novel she had been reading and also stuffed it into her bag. *The Silence of the Lambs.*

Stella shouldered the heavy bag and exited the Cone of Silence with me. "As a book lover, I always want the perfect happy ending."

CHAPTER 25

When we left the main branch, the stone lions were more courteous since I was accompanied by a famous librarian.

Stella wore a floppy, wide-brimmed hat along with a pair of large sunglasses. Despite her disguise, one lion perked up, sounding like a sycophant, "No books to check out today, Miss Artois?"

"Can I help you with anything, Miss Artois?" said the other.

"No, I was just enjoying some reading time. Don't want to call any attention to myself."

She walked with me down several of the large stone steps toward the street, then turned to look wistfully back up at the imposing stone edifice, where a gargoyle squatted above the gutters, skimming a sports magazine. She spoke in a distant voice, as if forgetting I was there. "I used to complain that not enough people were reading ... but at least they were *people*." She glanced at me, expecting a sympathetic ear. "I could enjoy ghost stories, monster stories, alien stories because it was all just fiction. I never meant to change the whole world."

As we descended the stone stairs, I felt I had to speak my mind. "I was a private investigator, ma'am, and I was killed on the job. That would have been the end of my story, a stand-alone with a dead detective in the end. Instead, it turned into a continuing series of adventures, all because of the Big Uneasy." I tapped the bullet hole in my forehead. "All because of you."

I looked out to see the people on the city sidewalk below, shoppers and businessmen, a group of unnatural school-children on a field trip, an invisible man in a raincoat and baseball cap.

Stella's expression soured as she remembered my zombie state of being. "I appreciate your perspective, Mr. Shamble." She patted her heavy book bag and changed the subject in embarrassment. She hurried down the stone steps. "I promise I'll get these sheets back to the publisher before the deadline."

In front of us, three prim women strutted along the side-walk. They wore high buttoned boots, long pleated skirts, whalebone corsets, and lacy cuffs. Their gentlemen escorts wore top hats, frock coats, flamboyant orange cravats. Two of the men had pointed goatees, and one sported an extravagant handlebar mustache. The women held parasols, and the men carried swagger sticks with polished brass heads.

The Olde Tymers. Worried that they might cause a scene, I moved closer to my companion. She wore her prominent disguise. How did anyone know that Stella had come to the library? No doubt some celebrity spotter was stalking her movements and taking photos for the tabloids.

Parked in front of a fire hydrant only twenty feet away was a completely different anachronism: a psychedelic van that looked as if it had driven fast enough to break through a time portal from the Summer of Love. The swirls of bright colors reminded me of the smoke wafting out of a hookah den. The Olde Tymers waited near the Scooby-Doo van as if expecting something.

Something else caught Stella's attention, though. She waved to a greenish-brown blob that was oozing and glurtching toward us. The shapeless mass had several brown-wrapped packages on his hump, held in place with a bungee cord. Mr. Latinous had apparently purchased the miniature train set Stella had wanted.

Not far from the psychedelic van, the three old-fashioned women twirled their parasols and lowered them like weapons into place. The tops had been painted with bold, black letters. *Remember G-O-D.*

In shrill voices they shouted, "For the good old days!"

The three gentlemen unsheathed their swagger sticks to reveal sword canes and waved the blades in the air. "There she is! Grab her."

The side door of the Scooby van popped open to reveal two more thugs hunched inside, dressed in old-fashioned hooligan outfits. The thugs sprang out of the van, each one holding a net. "One entangled librarian coming up!"

The van started up with a roar, coughing out greasy gray exhaust that no environmentally conscious hippie would have allowed.

Now Stella noticed them, and she screamed, "Help!"

I pulled out my .38. "Stay by me, Miss Artois. I'll protect you."

Two of the dapper men fell upon me, thrashing with their sword canes. I blocked one with my forearm, which would surely leave a bruise. Good thing my standing appointment at Bruno & Heinrich's Embalming Parlor was coming up soon.

I fired the pistol, intending it as a warning shot. The bullet went through the nearest man's top hat, leaving a neat, round hole, much like the one in my own forehead. The dapper attacker staggered backward, more indignant than frightened.

On top of the library steps, the fearsome lion statues rose up on their pedestals, snarling, but we had left the library property, and their range would not let them give assistance. People on the street stopped to stare at the commotion, and I hoped somebody had the common sense to call the police.

Stella screamed again and swung her heavy book bag, which knocked one of the Victorian women flat. As the librarian yelled, all along the main street, a series of manhole covers blasted into the air, flying up like frisbees and crashing down onto parked cars. I couldn't figure out what had caused it.

One of the hooligans threw his net at her, but it only caught the bulky book bag.

I was busy fighting off the next sword cane. Two of the women bustled in with their parasols in a secondary attack.

I fired another round from my .38, but the supposed gentleman smacked my wrist with his weaponized swagger stick hard enough to knock the gun out of my grasp.

The second hooligan threw his net, this time entangling Stella. I was sure the Olde Tymers meant to abduct the celebrity librarian for their own nefarious, if old-fashioned, purposes.

Then a blast of magical wind knocked us all backward, hurling the Victorian women flat on their bustles. I tried to figure out where the onslaught had come from, but before I could find any answers, a tsunami of snot crashed in, squelching and heaving itself upon the attackers. The bungee cords disconnected with a twang, and the twine-wrapped packages clattered onto the ground.

Then the mound of mucous was upon the nearest hooligan, engulfing him in unpleasant congestion. G. Latinous extended a pseudopod to bat aside the dapper gentlemen with sword canes. The Victorian women dropped their parasols and screamed as loudly as their corseted lungs would allow.

The blob consultant raised his shapeless body to form a protective mucous barrier that kept Stella Artois safe.

The Scooby van driver yelled from the rolled-down window, "Get out of here! Abort!"

The ladies in pleated dresses dove headfirst into the side door of the van, followed by the hooligans and gentlemen until everyone had crowded into the cargo area, where the seats had been removed for extra kidnapping room. The psychedelic van belched more unwholesome exhaust, and the nearly bald tires spun on the pavement as the vehicle squealed away.

Police sirens wailed in the distance, but too far away to help at the moment.

Even louder were the strangled gurgling sounds from the thug they had left behind. G. Latinous rolled off the subdued hooligan, leaving him covered with slime. His costume looked as if it had gone through a rinse cycle with used motor oil. His hair stuck out in globs, seemingly moussed with phlegm.

I held the .38 on him, daring him to move.

Meanwhile, Stella tugged at the net and finally pulled it off herself, which dislodged her hat and sunglasses. "Ruffian!" she snapped at him.

Definitely a better term than hooligan.

The ruffian seemed insulted. "We were just kidnapping. And for a good cause."

I started the interrogation even before the police showed up. "What cause?"

"To undo the Big Uneasy. It's her fault!" He jabbed an ooze-encrusted arm toward Stella. "She caused it all."

"Don't you think I'd undo it if I could?" Stella's eyes blazed with anger as she retorted. "It was an accident."

"How is kidnapping this woman going to undo the Big Uneasy?" I asked. "The *Necronomicon* caused it, not her."

The ruffian looked befuddled. "Oh. You mean we should have gone after the book?"

While the slime-drenched ruffian sulked on the sidewalk, Stella picked up the net that had entangled her and tossed it over the top of his head.

Turning from him, she faced the shifting, burbling blob. "You saved me, Mr. Latinous."

"I will add it to my bill as 'additional services rendered.'" He raised a lump so he could look down in disappointment at the cluttered packages on the ground. One had broken open, spilling tiny train parts, little houses and trees, sections of tracks, but the components were disarrayed rather than damaged.

I helped the blob gather the scattered model parts, tiny-gauge tracks and a little crossing light, and put them back into the box, then piled the boxes onto his back and secured them with the bungee cords.

"Let me escort you home, Miss Artois," G. offered.

The police sirens were much louder now.

"Thank you. I'll feel safer that way." She shouldered the heavy book bag and threw a withering sneer at the captive Olde Tymer, then strutted off with her consultant, leaving me to deal with the UQPD.

CHAPTER 26

t was dark by the time I got back to the offices after a very long day ... only to find the place quiet and empty. Too quiet.

That wasn't good. Had the same neighborhood-snatching sorcery occurred here at Chambeaux & Deyer?

I began searching, calling out names, and quickly saw it was a false alarm. Sheyenne had left a note on her desk explaining that she and Alvina had gone out for ice cream. Robin also wrote that she was taking case files home, where she planned to burn the midnight oil in preparing a brief on her cyclops double-vision case.

Relieved, I could relax and enjoy the tomb-like silence of the empty offices, maybe even get some reading done.

Mary Celeste's missing Elm Street case had been solved, in its own way, and she was back home and secure, though I still didn't have any real answers. I hadn't seen any obvious connections to Hairy Harry's vanished neighbors, but the two mysteries must be entangled somehow.

What did the ambi-polydextrous woman and the rogue werewolf cop have in common?

Mary was just an innocent girl trying to hit the big time as a hand model. I doubted she had any enemies. Why would anyone target Elm Street for erasure? None of her restored neighbors had seemed dangerous, or even interesting.

Hairy Harry, on the other hand, had pissed off a lot of people throughout his career—criminals he had busted, corrupt politicians and councilmen he had exposed, superiors he had beaten up. And that meant I had a whole Unnatural Quarter full of possible suspects.

Hairy had accidentally killed his partner Amy Littlemiss. Did the tragically shot rookie have a vengeful family? Someone with dark magic or necromancy? Could they have contracted an unnatural hit that depopulated his entire street?

Maybe Hairy Harry had only escaped because he was out walking the dog.

Maybe Mary had escaped because she'd been out late in a club, dancing the night away.

But what did a vendetta against Hairy Harry have to do with peaceful Elm Street?

I needed to know more about the rogue cop's sordid past, and the best way to get up to speed was to read his uncensored, and unedited, memoir. I'd read between the lines for clues and also, being a thorough P.I., I would read the actual lines themselves.

Hairy's new manuscript sat on the corner of my desk, almost as thick as the autograph sheets I had delivered to Stella Artois. It was going to be a long night.

I frowned at the curdled scum left at the bottom of my coffee mug and went into the kitchenette, intending to brew another pot, but I was brought up short by the profanity-laced threats the malevolent mold had written all over the wall. Clearly, Sheyenne's battle with the angry spores had escalated.

Not wanting to get involved in the office feud, I set my dirty mug on the counter and backed away from the kitchen. I would read Hairy Harry's tell-all book without the benefit of caffeine.

I sat down in my creaking chair, feeling my creaking joints. I definitely needed a top off of embalming fluid, and I checked the calendar for my standing appointment with Bruno & Heinrich—two days hence, an afternoon at the embalming emporium.

For now, I picked up the first page of the supposedly scandalous manuscript and started reading.

Hairy Harry wasn't the best writer, and his anger and self-righteousness came through with every paragraph, every adjective, every bit of unnecessary punctuation. He said he could spot "punks" from a mile away, identifying their guilt through keen lycanthropic senses, as well as his preformed opinions.

He loathed bureaucracy and ranted about injustice, giving examples that were clear (to him). He went on for pages about scumbag perps who got off with a slap on the wrist, and innocent victims who got no restitution at all.

I skimmed a bit.

He described violent clashes with his superiors on the UQ police force. He had fought city hall and brought down tainted politicians as well as gangsters, hit men, money launderers, and jaywalkers. He had broken up gambling rings; he had threatened dog owners who didn't clean up poop on the sidewalks. He took great enjoyment each time he growled his catchphrase, "Make my day!"

I skipped chapter eight and his torrid affair with the vampire coroner, not interested in a furry romance. Although … jilted lovers did make good suspects, especially an unnatural woman who might have magical powers or wizardly connections. So, I went back to chapter eight and read all the sex scenes, paying careful attention for clues.

The turning point of Hairy Harry's story was the tragic loss of his rookie partner. He wrote in deep cathartic detail about the fateful raid on the black-market Hummel warehouse, the shoot-out with the mummy mobster that had killed Amy Littlemiss. Hairy Harry had howled in outrage and despair, and Lenny Linens managed to escape. For a time.

After the incident, during an internal affairs review, the rogue cop was put on administrative leave. But relaxing and recovering did not make Hairy Harry's day. Instead, he hunted down Lenny Linens and delivered his own magnum-force justice.

First he incapacitated, or decapitated, the mobster's thugs, but he saved the best for the mafia mummy. He tracked down Lenny Linens after midnight, loping after him through an industrial district. The mummy fled, shooting at Hairy Harry, but he had foolishly neglected to load his weapon with silver bullets. Each minor wound only made the werewolf angrier.

Hairy Harry chased Lenny down a dark side street to a dead end at a drainage canal filled with brownish sludge. The desiccated mummy raised his claw-like hands in surrender, but the rogue cop knocked him into the water and forced the mummy to float there, flailing and splashing.

After enough time, the desiccated corpse had rehydrated, his flesh plumping up with moisture. While his skin and tissues swelled up, the linen wrappings around his throat and head remained the same size. Ultimately, the rehydrated Lenny Linens strangled to death on his own bandages.

Hairy Harry had felt vindicated. When the police chief found out what had happened, he reprimanded the werewolf cop. Lenny Linens's soggy, bloated body had been taken to the medical examiner's office in an attempt to restore him. But the sexy vampire coroner—who still had a thing for Hairy Harry—"mistakenly" let the mummy dry out much too long under a high-intensity heat lamp, reducing the evil mobster to a pile of dust and ashes, not enough to fill even a single canopic jar.

Revenge notwithstanding, the loss of poor Officer Little-miss had broken Hairy Harry. He suffered nightmares and daymares. He saw a psychologist, who diagnosed him with severe PTSD. After his darkest days, the therapist gave him a service animal, the hellhound Lucky. Hairy Harry wrote how much he loved the little puppy, how his damaged heart had at last begun to heal.

As I read page after page, the rogue cop pulled on my empathy, and I realized that this was meant to be a redemption story. He ended the book vowing to finish his journey on the road to recovery, so he could go bash some more punks.

The office door opened, and I expected to see Alvina and Sheyenne back from the ice cream parlor, but McGoo stood there with thumbs hooked through his belt loops. "Where is everybody, Shamble?" A shadow of concern crossed his face. "They weren't all teleported, were they?"

"No, just ice cream and legal briefs." I indicated the manuscript on my desk. "Meanwhile, I'm reading Hairy Harry's memoirs."

McGoo's eyes lit up. "I've heard so many stories about that guy! Everyone on the force talks about him." He lowered his voice. "Though we're not supposed to emulate his behavior. We've all been through sensitivity training, and Hairy Harry's exploits are used as examples—bad examples." He picked up the first few pages from the stack. "Can I read this? Sounds juicy."

I took the manuscript away and slid it into a desk drawer. "Sorry, client confidentiality. But you can order the first self-published version online. He'd be happy for the sale."

McGoo scoffed. "As if a famous guy like that would notice one sale!"

"Oh, he would."

The main phone rang, and I punched in. "Chambeaux & Deyer Investigations. How may I help you?"

"It's me again, punk!" The growling voice was easily recognizable.

"I was just reading your new memoir, sir. Very compelling."

"And now I have to add a whole new chapter—the part about the missing neighbors. Now they're all restored! Just reappeared, as if nothing happened."

McGoo was grinning and starstruck as he heard the loud voice. "Is that Hairy Harry himself?"

In the background I could hear the hellhound's barking and baying. Hairy Harry shouted, "Quiet, Lucky!" He came back on the line. "Look, Shamble, everyone's back, pretending to be normal."

"Pretending?"

"In a very suspicious and weird way. The neighbors are back in their driveways, on the sidewalk, in their lawns. Cooking dinner. Doing laundry, as if they were never gone! But they're too damn cheerful, as if they all feel safe or something. It's just not natural."

"Well, they are unnaturals," I pointed out.

"Not the same thing, punk!" Lucky continued baying at a high enough volume to knock the house off its concrete foundation. "Can you hear that?"

"All I hear is your hellhound."

"That's the point, punk! Everybody can hear it—and nobody's complaining! Any other time, my neighbors call me, leave notes, file grievances with the homeowners association.

Lucky's just being a puppy, and I can't stop him from barking. What am I supposed to do?"

"I'm glad they're not complaining now," I said.

"But it's damn weird they're not complaining! When I confronted the couple next door about them disappearing, they said they were just off on errands, but they wouldn't explain. It's not right, Shamble! Not right at all."

The rogue werewolf's words were loud enough to fill the office. "I'll go take a look," McGoo whispered to me. "I want to meet him!"

I said into the phone, "I'm sending my associate over, Mr. Harry. Someone with a fresh eye."

"Hurry up!"

McGoo snatched the spare self-published copy of *Make My Day* from my desk. "I'll pay you back later, Shamble. I'm going to get his autograph."

CHAPTER 27

The rest of the night was uneventful, and I didn't hear back from McGoo, so I assumed he had enjoyed his fanboy evening. Sheyenne and Alvina came back from ice cream, and we put the kid to bed in her air-conditioner box so she could get a good sleep, since she would be off to McGoo's the following night.

The next day in the office, though, I faced a new challenging task—giving Alvina a pop quiz from her mad-scientist chemistry homework.

Not surprisingly, my half-daughter is a genius. She got every question correct about acids, bases, alchemy, and astrology, even an extra-credit question on advanced molecular-level goop formulation. Earlier, Alvina had aced the do-it-yourself final exam in the *Estate Law for Children* workbook that Robin had assigned.

"You show aptitude in a lot of different subjects, kid," I said.

Alvina flashed her pointy smile at me. "I'm considering different career possibilities. Being a mad scientist sounds like fun, and knowing chemistry could help me get a job at the Monster Chow Factory or Jekyll Necroceuticals, if they ever get back in business." She perked up. "Or I could use my sophisticated chemistry knowledge to become a bartender! I could work at the Goblin Tavern."

"The sky's the limit," I said.

"We might find even better alternatives than those, honey," Sheyenne said, coming to help.

With the quiz finished, we flipped to the next chapter in the workbook, for hours of fun-at-home mad-scientist activities. This week's laboratory unit covered toxic substances, high-energy explosives, and lingering poisons. There was a special sidebar for Friends and Family.

While I read aloud the section on how caustic chemicals or radioactive substances could create useful mutants, Sheyenne gathered household materials for the lab exercise. She fetched bottles from the refrigerator, under the bathroom sink, and even Renfeld's janitorial closet.

As Sheyenne brought out beakers, measuring spoons, funnels, and a tarnished old spoon, I kept thinking about my current cases, particularly Hairy Harry's now un-missing neighbors. I wished McGoo had called to tell me what he had found, but he isn't great at follow up. After the end of his shift, he'd probably stopped off at the tavern for a quick beer, which had turned into a slow second beer, and then home to sleep, or maybe clean up for Alvina.

With her laboratory notebook open beside the bottles and jars of foul-smelling chemicals, Alvina read the assignment instructions, checked off the ingredients.

Following the steps, Alvina poured gray sludge into brown sludge, then added bright green antifreeze and a cup of bleach. Foam bubbled up in an angry, steaming, snarling reaction. Smoke twisted out, brown and fiery orange mixed with magenta.

Alvina giggled. Robin quietly closed her office door to block the noxious and possibly mutagenic fumes. I was glad I didn't need to breathe.

The frothing experiment spurted up a jet of yellow smoke

and sparkles. Alvina was delighted. "That's for extra-credit points!"

Before the caustic substance could make a mess on our main table, Sheyenne used her poltergeist powers to whisk the chemistry homework toward the kitchen.

I called after her. "Careful dumping that down the sink. It might eat away the pipes."

"Not going to waste it down the sink, Beaux—I'm using it on the mold!"

Alvina trotted after her.

Then McGoo entered the office, clad in a fresh, clean blue uniform. "Just thought I'd stop by on my rounds."

His hair was neatly in place beneath his cap, and his expression was calm. He gave me a pleasant smile, rather than the usual horse-like grin that told me he had discovered a new joke. He looked clean-cut, well-groomed, and—dare I say it —*professional*. I wondered what the occasion was.

"Hey, McGoo," I said. "I didn't hear back from you after you saw Hairy Harry. Did you get your book autographed?"

He gave me a bland look. "It's all fine."

The chemistry fumes still hung in the air like a thundercloud made of bruises. I waved my hand to swirl away the vapors, surprised McGoo didn't make a "Who farted?" wisecrack.

"Sorry about the stink," I explained. "Alvina's doing her mad-scientist chemistry lab work."

He walked to the window on the far wall. "Here, I'll let in some fresh air." He was being helpful, and that made me suspicious.

"Are you all right, McGoo?" With a tinge of dread I added, "Is there some other bad news? Did you ... hear from Rhonda?"

He shook his head. "Haven't heard from Rhonda in a while. I doubt she'll cause any more trouble."

Very odd. "So, tell me what happened at Hairy Harry's. Everybody returned safe and sound? No evidence of tele-portation?"

"None whatsoever. The street checked out. The people are home, and the neighborhood is back to normal. Case closed."

My frown deepened. "You're not even going to make a joke?"

"Nothing to joke about." He paused as if trying to remember something. "Oh, can you please take care of our daughter for one more night? I got offered an extra shift on patrol, and I'd like the few extra hours."

McGoo volunteering for an extra shift?

"You sure there's nothing wrong?" I pressed.

We heard a pop and sputter from the kitchenette, and more noxious smoke burbled out. Alvina squealed with laughter, and she and Sheyenne retreated. Both of them looked disheveled (and it's difficult to dishevel a ghost). "We sure taught that mold some manners," Sheyenne said with a huff. "If Alvina's new toxic cleaner doesn't work, I'm going to file a fungal tres-passing charge."

"Happy to help you do the paperwork if you choose to go that route," McGoo offered. "Once you've exhausted all stan-dard routes of mediation."

Now Alvina brightened as she saw him. "There's my half-daddy! Are you here to pick me up already?" She looked at the clock on the wall.

"We'll be keeping you tonight, kid," I said. "He's got an extra shift on patrol."

Even Alvina looked startled by the idea.

McGoo tipped his officer's cap and turned back to the door. "Thanks again for the help, Shamble. I owe you one."

"You owe me a lot," I said. "But who's keeping track?"

He didn't even grin as he left the office.

Sheyenne, Alvina, and I looked at each other, puzzled. McGoo seemed normal for the first time since I'd known him.

CHAPTER 28

Even a zombie detective needs to get his hands dirty sometimes. I decided to investigate Hairy Harry's street myself.

McGoo's surprisingly un-erratic behavior could have been sparked by something he'd seen or encountered the night before. When it comes to friends, you can't be too suspicious.

As I grabbed my jacket and fedora, Alvina finished an additional homework assignment that Sheyenne graded with a bright red A. The kid hopped down from her chair. "I'm going with you."

I shook my head. "Too dangerous."

"You said it was too normal." She put on a pleading face. "I've got a proposal for Mr. Harry. Remember, I'm his social-media expert and marketing savant."

"Savant?" I asked.

"It's one of the new words I learned in English class."

A faint haze of chemistry-homework fumes still lingered even with the window open, but most had dissipated. I glanced at Alvina's laptop resting among the scattered papers. "Do you have a marketing printout to show him?"

She frowned, as if she had just swallowed mustard-flavored blood. "A printout? Like, on paper? That sucks." She held up her phone. "I have slideshows with subsidiary links, and a spreadsheet with projected demographics, even a full-fledged

Monstagram campaign that'll bump up sales on his old indie-published edition of *Make My Day*."

"That one's outdated. Hairy Harry gave me a new manuscript," I said. "An expanded version with even more controversial details."

The girl's eyes were so bright I could barely see the bloodshot lines. "Right, that's why we have to sell the original version now. We'll capture the names of first-time customers and market the expanded version to them because they're self-identified as Hairy Harry fans."

"And then we take down the old version?" I just didn't understand these things.

Alvina seemed exasperated. "No, then we keep marketing it as the classic original version, uncut and unedited."

"Might not want to advertise that it's unedited."

"Pleeeeease? Can I please go along? I want to see him—and meet his hellhound."

I'm not good at withstanding persistent half-daughter pressure. "If the problem is that everyone's too normal, then I suppose the risk can't be too high."

Since I had grudgingly agreed to pass along the expanded manuscript to Mavis and Alma Wannovich, I suggested we could stop at the publishing offices on the way. Alvina bounced up and down with excitement.

I made a call to Mavis, but when I explained, she and her sow sister offered to join us at Hairy Harry's house instead, since they very much wanted to meet the famous rogue cop themselves.

I shrugged. "The more the merrier." The extra company would provide safety in numbers and also additional witnesses.

It was a nice, gloomy day, so I decided to walk, which

would give Alvina a chance to burn off some excess energy. She hopped and skipped all the way to Hairy Harry's now-repopulated neighborhood.

On the corner we met up with Mavis in her pleated black dress and pointy hat. Alma snuffled in the gutters, then squealed when she saw us, prancing on her trotters. Alvina wrapped her arms around the sow. "You are so cute! Piggy, piggy!"

Heading over to the werewolf's house, I briefed the Wannovich sisters about the kidnapping attempt on Stella Artois at the library. Both were appalled by the attempted crime, but I reassured them the celebrity librarian was fine, and that I had managed to deliver the signature sheets.

Mavis made a sour face. "I don't understand those Olde Tymers. How can they not enjoy the changes in the world? If they gave me half a chance, I'd cast a spell and make them happy with magic." Alma snorted, and Mavis nodded at her sister. "I agree, dear. Things are so much better now."

Since the big sow had once been a normal witch, I was surprised she believed her situation was improved from before. Maybe there were unexpected advantages to being a pig. Not everyone is as comfortable in their own skin.

The kid took on a more professional demeanor as she faced the witch sisters. "I'm glad you'll get a chance to meet Mr. Harry in person, but keep in mind that I'll be the one formally pitching his book to you. I'm his agent."

"Yes, dear. You told us in the offices," Mavis said.

Alvina continued, "*Make My Day* is a true story about injustice and redemption."

"And action," I added. "Lots of shootouts and car chases."

Mavis offered a pleased smile. "Any good redemption story

needs shootouts and car chases, in my professional editorial opinion. And I hear there's sex, too."

Everyone gave us neighborly waves as we walked down the street, hearing only the buzz of pleasant conversation, a lawn gnome using a tiny trowel to plant petunias, an orc in a mail-carrier's uniform strolling along with a heavy mail satchel. Brassy Mexican music came from an old boombox next to a zombie patiently charring hotdogs on a charcoal grill. Alma lifted her snout in the air as she smelled the hotdogs, and let out a grunt of disapproval.

Hairy Harry sat outside on his porch, half-watching a base-ball game on an old portable TV. The enormous black hell-hound rolled around on the brown front lawn, waving his massive paws in the air, wagging his tail. I expected to hear earsplitting yowls, but when Lucky saw us coming, his ears just pricked up. He didn't make so much as a whimper or a bark.

"Good dog," Alvina said.

"Careful," I told her, but the vampire girl was fearless. She scratched behind the hound's giant ears, careful not to impale herself on the spiked collar. Lucky thumped his tail in a sedate metronome. His tongue lolled out, and slobber dripped onto the grass, leaving deeper brown stains.

The witch sisters and I approached the rogue cop. Slouched in the lawn chair, Hairy Harry reached over to turn down the TV volume.

"After your call last night I was concerned, sir." I looked around. "I came to check on you."

"Nice afternoon." The werewolf's voice wasn't much of a growl, and he didn't even call me punk.

I pressed, "You sounded alarmed on the phone, and Lucky wouldn't stop barking."

"Oh, he's stopped now. No complaints from the neighbors." He waved his paw to the zombie at the barbecue grill, who waved back. "Perfect little neighborhood here."

When the sow snorted for attention, I remembered my manners. "Mr. Harry, I want to introduce you to Mavis and Alma Wannovich, editors at Howard Phillips Publishing."

Mavis stepped forward. "We've heard so much about your new manuscript! With the self-published edition, you may have already reached your immediate fan base, but we could use your ... agent's marketing efforts to expand the audience with a new, authorized edition."

Leaving the hellhound, Alvina ran up to the porch. "My new Monstagram campaign is all worked out. I have a whole presentation." She held up her phone, ready to show him, but the werewolf wasn't interested. After an awkward moment, she said, "I can Airdrop it to you."

"I'm sure you did a good job, girl," Hairy Harry said.

The sow snorted, and Mavis translated, "Now, we have to review the manuscript first before we make any editorial decisions. Your agent will send it forthwith, but we wanted to meet you face-to-face to open a dialog."

The rogue cop glanced at the muted TV to check the score of the ballgame. "Sorry to waste your time. That book was just a bunch of nonsense, me venting, stroking my own ego."

We were all surprised by his attitude. Alvina looked particularly crestfallen.

"Just a silly indulgence," he continued. "Who'd want to read my memoirs anyway?"

"You said the whole world needed to read them," I said. "And you told me they were dangerous."

"Dangerous?" With a claw, he picked a morsel of food from between his fangs. "I suppose you might get a papercut from it

—and these days, we all know how dangerous papercuts can be, at the wrong time and place." He turned up the volume on the television, distracted by the game. "Thanks for stopping by."

After a long awkward silence, we all left. Mavis seemed the most concerned, looking suspiciously at the werewolf's house, his neighbors. Her inner alarm bells were going off about something.

She picked up the pace, breathing hard by the time we turned the corner and got back to a more normal unnatural street. "Something is not right here, Mr. Shamble. You say his neighborhood vanished and returned … but this does not seem to be the same neighborhood as before."

"Or the same Hairy Harry," I added. "An identical thing happened on Elm Street. Very peculiar."

Alvina's eyes were filled with concern. We were both reminded of how McGoo had changed, too.

"They're like bad photocopies." Mavis bustled along in her black sensible boots. Sweat had appeared on her forehead. "Let's go somewhere we can talk in private. This is important. I think I might know what's happening."

CHAPTER 29

onsidering the look of abject fear on the witch's face, I decided to take us to the Ghoul's Diner, where we would be safe (although perhaps not from the food). The diner was a public place where we could discuss the imaginary dangers we faced. It would be oddly crowded, considering the quality of the menu, but at least we wouldn't be stalked or attacked there.

As we hurried toward the entrance, Mavis tugged her wide-brimmed black hat down and hunched her shoulders. "Keep a low profile," she whispered. She seemed to think no one would recognize her black dress and steel-wool hair.

I whispered back, "What exactly are we worried about? Hairy Harry's street seemed perfectly bland."

"Too bland!" Mavis leaned closer. "I don't think it's the original neighborhood at all, but a cheap copy. Quick, let's get inside!"

Alvina treated this like a grand adventure, and she pulled open the door. Intimidating smells curled up like greasy fumes. Customers of all stripes, shapes, and flavors sat at the flecked counter or in upholstered booths.

"I'll order breakfast cereal," said Alvina. "They open a good box of Unlucky Charms."

"Wouldn't you rather have bacon and eggs? They put swirls of ketchup on the sunny-side up eggs so they look like bloodshot eyes." When Alma snorted uncomfortably, I amended, "Okay, we'll skip the bacon."

Two werewolves hunched on stools at the counter, picking hair from their salads. In the nearest booth, a giant mother fly slurped up a plate of the carrion special, then leaned over, opened her articulated mouth, and regurgitated the food into the squealing mouths of her larvae. A group of vampire businessmen had pushed two tables together and squabbled over how to split the check, while Esther the harpy waitress snapped at them to hurry up. She fluffed her plumage and paced with taloned feet, anxious to take her break.

Albert Gould, the owner, slaved over boiling cauldrons, hot stoves, fermenting bins, and a decaying pot. Albert wasn't the most personable guy, but he was chatty enough for a ghoul.

Alvina picked an empty booth, although the table was still cluttered with dirty dishes. She scooted across the upholstered cushion. Mavis slid into the booth next to Alvina, still trying not to be noticed. The sow curled up under the table.

I eased myself in beside the witch. "Is this a safe enough place? Can we talk here?"

Furtive, Mavis narrowed her eyes. "Nowhere's safe, if what I fear is true. Any of these people could be someone else."

I raised my eyebrows. "We don't know who they are in the first place. They look like strangers to me."

"I think they're duplicates," she said. "Doppelgangers! Exact copies."

I couldn't help but think of the alarming change not only in Hairy Harry and Lucky and in Mary Celeste's neighbors, but also in my best human friend. I also remembered the odd warning Linda Bullwer had given me after being attacked by the pit bull dogwood tree. "What exactly do you mean by doppelgangers? Isn't one set of monsters good enough?"

"A replacement set," Mavis said.

"Oh, like *Invasion of the Body Snatchers*," said Alvina. I was surprised the kid knew about the movie, and she explained, "I've been studying the classics."

I leaned closer to Mavis. "You're suggesting that Mr. Harry's whole neighborhood vanished and then returned as bad copies? Same with Elm Street? But if those people were replaced, what happened to the originals?"

Alvina asked in a hushed voice, "Did you check for pods?"

Esther sauntered up to the booth, ready to take our order or to get into an argument. Sniffing in annoyance at the dirty dishes on the table, she rearranged the half-empty water glasses and left them in front of us, then swept away the dirty plates. With a huff she demanded, "What do you want?"

"I'll have Unlucky Charms, please," Alvina said. "And extra milk. I like how it turns red."

"No longer serving breakfast," the harpy said.

"Then I'll have the dinner special of Unlucky Charms." Alvina stared down Esther, and I could see it was going to be a long face-off.

Behind the counter, Albert the ghoul saw me and slurred out, "Shamble." He put a plate under the heat lamp, where it bubbled and oozed like a failed experiment. "Special ..."

"Just having coffee today, Albert," I said. Even that was a risk.

"Bad coffee," the ghoul replied.

"I know. I've had it before."

Esther gave me a withering glare. "Coffee, that's all? What's the matter, can't afford anything else?"

"Just coffee for now, Esther," I repeated. She had waited on me enough times that I knew not to provoke her.

Mavis shook her head. "Nothing for me, thanks." She tugged her hat even lower. "I'm not here."

Insulted as always, Esther stalked off.

In the back I heard a spray of water and a clatter of dishes. Mary worked at the steaming industrial dishwasher, dressed in a stained wet apron, her hair a mess. With a pressure nozzle, she sprayed off plates and silverware in a flurry of hands and arms, stacking, rinsing, rearranging. She held coffee mugs in three of her hands, but managed to wave at us with the fourth.

Without even turning in our order, Esther plopped down at a tiny table near the smoldering coffee station. "I'm on my break!" She made sure everyone knew not to demand service for the next half hour.

Mary sprayed a load of dishes and rolled it into the washing vault. "I'll take care of the dining room, Albert. I can serve the customers."

Albert lifted his head to look at her as if he couldn't comprehend what she was suggesting. "But Esther's the waitress," he said, either a statement or a warning.

As the dishwashing machine continued to rinse and roar, Mary removed her suds-soaked apron and tied on a perky little waitress apron instead. "I'm looking to move my way up, get a raise." We already knew she was a plucky young woman.

"Let's see what Esther has to say about that," I muttered.

Mary strutted out, snagged a coffeepot in one of her hands as the harpy waitress stared at her in disbelief. The multi-armed woman sashayed over to me with a mug and an urn of the foul, dark coffee. "I've worked a day and a half straight, Mr. Shamble. I just want to sleep, but I'm not really comfortable going home. It still doesn't feel right there."

"Doppelgangers," Mavis said in a stage whisper.

Back in the corner booth, I was surprised to see a

familiar figure slouched low. Linda Bullwer sat with her notepad, pretending not to watch us, and jotting down notes.

"Doppelgangers?" Mary gave Mavis a questioning look. Before the witch could answer, her sow sister squealed a warning from underneath the table.

Esther stormed over, her feathers ruffled. "How dare you steal my customers! You're a low-class dishwasher. Get your hands off my tips."

The four-armed young woman did not respond well to bitchiness. "*Your* tips? A person has to *work* for tips, and you aren't taking care of these customers."

"Shamble is my customer," Esther snarled.

Both defiant women looked at me, insisting that I make a choice. "I'm fine right now, thanks." I looked down at the bubbling ooze in the coffee cup. "I won't need a refill for a while."

"You had no right!" Esther shrieked at her. "I'm the waitress here."

"Albert's promoting me," Mary retorted.

Behind the counter, the ghoul looked sickened by the suggestion. "Could use another waitress ..."

"These people have all the service they can stand," the harpy cried.

Mary shocked us all by winding back all four arms and letting loose a quadruple succession of slaps across the waitress's face. Esther's expression was so astounded she deserved an Academy Award.

In the kitchen, the dishwasher finished its cycle and spilled out the steaming clean dishes. Albert said, "Need you back here, Mary."

The polydactyl, polydextrous young woman flounced back

to her station, taking just enough time to raise all four hands to Esther in a multiple one-finger salute.

Esther turned about, as if cowed. "I'll get your coffee, Shamble."

"And my Unlucky Charms," Alvina called, but the waitress didn't respond.

"Now everybody's watching us." Mavis hunched forward over the sticky booth table. "We need to get out of here as soon as we're finished. Alma and I will research how to fix this and develop a counterspell. Everyone in this diner could be a doppelganger."

"If we could replace Esther," I mumbled, "it wouldn't necessarily be bad."

CHAPTER 30

After listening to Mavis's suspicions about replacement neighborhoods and doppelgangers, my stomach felt queasy—and the Ghoul's Diner was only partly responsible.

Our group walked back together—safety in numbers. Alvina's lips were bright red from the food coloring in her Unlucky Charms, but I could tell she was disappointed that Hairy Harry was uninterested in her marketing proposals.

But was it the real werewolf cop, or a doppelganger?

I dropped the kid off at our offices, but decided it was important to escort the Wannoviches to the publishing head-quarters. The more those two talked about their conspiracy theory, the more paranoid they got.

"We're in the middle of something big," Mavis said. "And right now I'd rather be thinking small."

"If those people in the normal neighborhoods are just bad copies, is there a reversal spell?" I asked. "A body-snatcher repellant?"

"We have a complete library of spellbooks back in our editorial offices," Mavis said. "Alma and I will dig into it."

After seeing Linda Bullwer taking notes in the corner booth, I wondered if she knew something the rest of us didn't. She seemed to have a missing piece of the puzzle ... or maybe she was just concocting a subplot for her *Necronomicon* sequel.

A block away from the publishing skyscraper, G. Latinous glurped up to us from a side street. "Afternoon, neighbor," he said in his deep underwater voice.

"Out for a walk, Mr. Latinous?"

"It's hard to go for a walk when you don't have legs. But I am out for a casual … ooze."

I introduced the rolling mucous to the Wannovich sisters, but the witches weren't in a very sociable mood. They tried to make chitchat, but then came to a horrified halt when we turned the corner and came upon a large group of rowdy protesters around a bonfire in the pedestrian plaza by the front entrance. The shouting people wore old-fashioned clothes, accessorized with parasols, corsets, top hats, pocket watches, and other uncomfortable attire.

I looked for any of the ones who had tried to nab the celebrity librarian, but all Olde Tymers looked the same to me. I hadn't understood how they intended to unravel the Big Uneasy by kidnapping Stella Artois, nor did I understand what they meant to accomplish by building a fire in front of Howard Phillips Publishing.

The bonfire was composed of crackling, burning books— piled volumes that had been doused with lighter fluid and ignited. I saw an odd assortment of thick tomes and skinny pamphlets, hardcovers and paperbacks. The paper sent a corkscrew of smoke into the air as it was incinerated.

Despite their constrictive costumes, the Olde Tymers capered around the pyre like Ewoks at a sacrifice. With a whoop and a holler, a pair of Victorian-clad women dumped a complete set of the Shamble & Die mysteries into the flames, shouting, "Remember G-O-D!"

"Bring back the good old days!" yelled a man in a stovepipe hat.

I thought I recognized him from the kidnapping fiasco, but he wore a different frock coat, so I couldn't be sure.

"Oh, dearie," said Mavis. "We should use the back entrance." The sow let out a whimpering snort.

The blob slurched along with us, his coloration darkening with concern. I suggested to him, "G., you could just roll forward and swamp them all. That would be an effective use of congestion."

He quivered. "I may be a consultant, Mr. Shamble, but I will not be hired out to do violence. I prefer to avoid the conflict entirely."

His body mass shifted, and he glurped off toward the rear of the publishing building. He ducked down a side alley with a sewer grate and a large drainage pipe from the gutter above.

Then I saw McGoo at the edge of the plaza, calmly observing the protest in his full blue uniform. He was talking to a man in a charcoal-gray business suit, whom I recognized as Philip Phillips. Both of them just stared at the bonfire. Philip didn't even seem perturbed to see his own books rising up in flames.

A stream of the Olde Tymers entered the lobby bookstore, purchased armloads of various titles, paid a troll cashier, then headed back out to the plaza, where they threw the books onto the roaring blaze.

Philip gave a polite nod to me, Mavis, and Alma as we came up to ask them what was happening. Oddly, the publisher was smiling. "It's going to be a good sales day."

McGoo also acknowledged me, still professional, freshly shaven, all of which I found very odd. "Hey, Shamble."

That was it. No sarcastic comment, no rude observation.

Philip indicated the commotion and the bonfire. "They're

angry about our enhanced version of the *Necronomicon*. They blame that book for causing the Big Uneasy."

"They blame everything for causing the Big Uneasy, including Stella Artois," I said. "What have they got against the Shamble & Die mysteries? Should I be offended?"

"In their eyes, our entire imprint is tainted." Philip smiled as copies of *Unnatural Acts* and *Hair Raising* were thrown into the flames. "That's the last of our stock. Looks like we need to go into another printing."

My BHF seemed completely uninterested. I asked, "What are you doing here, McGoo?"

"Added security. By request." He made no move to stop the howling Olde Tymers from throwing more books onto the fire.

I was distracted by movement out of the corner of my eye. I saw the blob consultant disappear into the alley shadows. I expected him to take a shortcut down the sewer drainpipe, but instead I watched a blurp of his ooze disappear up the downspout.

I frowned. "The snot thickens ..."

Before I could investigate, the protesters grew louder and louder. An entire stack of the old, remaindered cookbook, *To Serve Man*, went up in smoke.

Then a loud alarm went off inside the building, a ringing bell, as if grade school had been called into session ... or a bank robbery had just taken place.

Philip gasped. "That's our high-security alert! But the offices are closed. We sent everyone home, locked the upper floors."

"What if someone's trying to steal our copyedited manuscripts?" Mavis cried.

The Olde Tymers were undoubtedly behind the mischief,

but the protesters seemed just as alarmed by the alarm. They used the racket as an excuse to jeer even louder and throw more books onto the fire.

McGoo made no move to respond until the publisher grabbed his arm. "Come, officer! Let's get inside the building and stop what's happening. You need to apprehend the perpetrators."

McGoo finally swung into motion. "Apprehend the perpetrators. That's in my job description."

We gave the bonfire a wide berth and rushed inside the lobby, past the line of protesters buying more books to burn, then to the elevator in back. The sow's bulk took up a lot of room in the elevator car, but we crowded together. Philip used an access key to take us directly to the thirteenth floor.

The doors slid open to reveal offices that were dim and quiet, except for the loud alarm bell and the flashing strobe lights. The work cubicles were empty, since all production, editing, and marketing was done for the day.

Mavis pointed ahead and whimpered. "It's gone. Oh no, it's gone!"

Alma grunted and squealed.

Philip gasped. "It was a rarity, one of a kind! Now it's stolen!"

The pedestal and display case that held the original *Necronomicon*—the sacred tome activated by one drop of virgin's blood from a paper cut—had been knocked over, the display-case lock cracked open.

The thick, rare book was gone.

McGoo showed little reaction, as if he were seeing nothing more than a parking violation.

I looked at him and quipped, "Necronomi-*gone*."

I thought it was a cute joke, but McGoo didn't even snicker.

Chapter 31

When the incessant alarm fell silent, my teeth finally stopped vibrating.

McGoo calmly tried to get us to leave. "Nothing to see here." He seemed oddly aloof about the audacious theft from right under our noses—well, actually from thirteen stories above our heads.

Mavis, however, made up for it with an excess of panic. "Of course there's nothing to see—someone stole the *Necronomicon*!" Alma snuffled for clues around the toppled display case.

Philip paced about, muttering. "It's a priceless book! We'd better not find it on eBay."

I tried to sound reassuring. "If that's the case, the thief won't be able to put up a listing right away. There's a whole process, taking photos, writing up a description, setting up a black-market account. We have time."

McGoo stared straight ahead. He could have been replaced by a cardboard standee of a cop, which might have been just as effective. I scratched my head. "McGoo, you're worrying me. Are you feeling all right?"

"I'm just the way I should be, Shamble."

In alarm, Mavis mouthed the word, "Doppelganger!"

In back, the heavy steel doors of the Executive offices

opened, and Howard hurried in, sweating and wide-eyed. "The security system said Code Blood Red. What happened?"

His twin gestured to the pedestal. "We are *Necronomicon*-less."

Howard sucked in a quick breath. "Then it's vital that we release our facsimile edition as soon as possible."

McGoo headed back to the elevator. "I've done all I can here. I'll leave you to it." He stepped in and closed the doors without further explanation.

Howard turned to me. "Mr. Shamble, we need to engage your services for additional security."

Philip cut in, "I authorize that we hire you as extra security on a contract basis. We're familiar with your work at Chambeaux & Deyer—both your real cases and the fictionalized ones."

Howard nodded in close consultation with his brother. "If the *Necronomicon* is gone, the most important thing we can do is gain publicity for the situation." He looked at his twin, and both nodded. "I'll make some calls, cash in a few favors."

"I hoped to reserve my best contacts for the actual book release," Philip said, "but this is a crisis."

Howard gave an even brisker nod. "We'll be on TV before sundown."

WRIP, the Unnatural Quarter's main public-access station, was a small TV studio with a simultaneous radio broadcast. Using the impressive loaner hearse, I escorted the Phillips brothers to their emergency 5:00 PM live interview. Howard and Philip sat in the back seat of the big vehicle (though not in the coffin cargo compartment). I didn't mind the role as chauffeur, so long as they didn't ask me to put on a tux. The funeral suit I'd worn for their book-launch gala was as fancy as I got.

WRIP was a drab, cinderblock building with skeletal antennae rising from the rooftop like an out-of-control erector set. Inside a fenced compound, satellite dishes looked like high-energy weapons for use against Godzilla or any lesser-known kaiju that happened to wander into the Quarter.

After the twin publishers emerged from the back seat, I pressed the studio's door intercom. "This is Dan Chambeaux, delivering Howard and Philip Phillips for an interview."

The lock disengaged with a loud clunk, and I let the twin publishers in. They looked very self-important. Howard leaned close to me and said, "Don't be nervous, Mr. Shamble."

Philip patted me on the back. "You'll do fine."

I didn't know what they meant.

The station's lobby was the size of a crypt and just as welcoming. The receptionist, a frowning gray gargoyle, asked us to sign in. "All three of you. I'll get your visitor badges." Her voice was as fresh as rock dust.

Howard and Philip jotted down their information, then handed me the clipboard. "You'll be coming in with us."

"You need security inside the studio?"

"We need *you* inside the studio," Philip said.

After the gargoyle receptionist pressed a button, the back door opened up. "The green room is first door on the left. Wait there."

TV guests could relax in the lounge before their big moment in the WRIP limelight. The walls were painted a sickly olive green with undertones of vomit. A battered brown sofa had all of its springs sprung, the cushions eviscerated by the claws of nervous interviewees. An old coffeemaker still had an inch of dark sludge left from the morning's brew, ten hours earlier. Howard picked up a Styrofoam cup. "Coffee, Mr. Chambeaux?"

I considered carefully. This liquid looked even worse than the java at the Ghoul's Diner. "No thanks. It might keep me awake all night."

Philip said, "Then you can work on our case."

"I thought I was providing security," I said.

"We'll hire you to find the *Necronomicon*, too," Howard offered. "If you can fit it in."

Philip quickly added, "It'll make a rollicking case for Miss Bullwer to include in an upcoming novel. You can talk about it on TV, but don't give any specifics."

I was suddenly wary. "Why am I talking on TV?"

Before they could answer, a harried human producer scuttled into the green room. She had a pen tucked behind one ear and an energy drink in her left hand. "Come quickly! Our 4:40 PM scheduled interview canceled at the last minute." She huffed. "A vampire historian got so excited about the show that he accidentally immolated himself in the blazing sun—and there's not much point in questioning a pile of ashes." She gestured to all three of us. "So, you're up next. Onto the set! We'll get you miked up. Makeup artist is already out there. Dick is ready for you as soon as we come out of commercial break."

I balked. "Excuse me? I'm not going on TV."

The producer huffed again. "Mister, I don't have time for more problems today. You're the zombie detective, right? The Phillips brothers promised us an exclusive interview with Dan Shamble himself."

"It's Dan *Chambeaux*," I corrected, the wheels spinning in my mind.

"Then why is the series called Shamble & Die? We already have our questions prepared on the teleprompter."

Howard raised a finger. "We would, of course, like to mention the recent theft of the *Necronomicon*."

"If there's time." The producer urged us out of the green room and down the hall to the set.

I asked the Phillips brothers, "But what am I supposed to talk about?"

"Just be yourself. The unnatural charm will come through, and then people will buy the books," Howard said.

"I thought we were here about the stolen *Necronomicon*."

"They needed a hook for the interview, and we needed publicity," Philip said. "No such thing as bad publicity. Dick the Head is a good interviewer, and he'll just throw a few softballs at you."

"I'm going to be talking to Dick the Head?"

Howard smiled. "I told you I have connections."

The set held a pair of potted artificial plants, three comfortable chairs, and a china platter to display the familiar decapitated head of the zombie commentator.

Howard and Philip came forward to greet the talk-show host. Despite the efforts of the studio makeup artist, Dick's skin was splotchy, and he needed a fresh dose of embalming fluid—as did I.

The head grinned at me. "Dan-O, glad to meet another prominent zombie. I'm Dick the Head—don't leave out the 'the'!" He chortled.

Assistants bustled around, clipping a small microphone to the collar of my bullet-ridden jacket, tucking a battery pack into my pocket, then trying to hide the cords in my shirt. Two others fussed over Howard and Philip.

"I'm very familiar with you, sir," I said to Dick. "You worked with my partner Robin Deyer in your legal case."

"Robin, of course! We need both of you for a candid interview, someday. She's as much a part of the Shamble & Die adventures as you are."

"Of course she is. But, uh, we're here for something much more important. The original *Necronomicon* has been stolen from Howard Phillips Publishing. The theft has some pretty serious repercussions."

Howard leaned closer to me. "When we talk about that, be sure to mention our special edition of the book. Can you put a preorder link on the scroll at the bottom of the screen?"

Dick the Head gave instructions to the control room.

"And be sure to spell my name correctly," I added.

I was unceremoniously shoved into one of the guest chairs, while a goblin makeup artist slathered my face with a coating of flesh-colored powder, then turned to the twin publishers. She groaned with dismay. "Crap, I put human flesh color on the wrong face! We'll just have to make do. No time." She proceeded to cover Howard and Philip with pale gray powder.

I felt awkward and uncomfortable, especially when I realized that Robin, Sheyenne, and Alvina often watched *Conversations with Dick the Head* in the afternoons. "I'll try not to embarrass myself."

"Leave the embarrassing to me, Dan-O," said Dick. "Just leave the embarrassing to me."

The cameras encroached like military weapons, and the bright lights shone on our faces. Perched on his china platter, Dick the Head came back from commercial break and launched right into introductions.

"Today we have a special guest, the rugged hero of the

Shamble & Die adventures." Dick the Head let out a false chuckle. "You've heard me talk about his partner Robin Deyer and her legal skills. Mr. Shamble is a zombie private investigator, and I hear he's hot on a new case. Tell us about the case, Dan-O!"

He stared at me, expecting me to jump in with an impromptu answer. "Yes, uh, there's been a disturbing theft at Howard Phillips Publishing. The original *Necronomicon* has vanished. It's possibly the most powerful book in the world. We wouldn't want it to fall into the wrong hands."

Philip leaned forward into the camera field, cutting in. "And you can read all about Mr. Shamble's adventures in the book series from Howard Phillips Publishing. The most recent collection is titled *Services Rendered*."

Howard interjected, "The loss of the original *Necronomicon* is a tragedy, but we are proud to announce that our company will release an amazing collector's edition of the *Necronomicon* for the twelfth anniversary of the Big Uneasy."

Philip flashed his twin brother an annoyed glance. "Delayed by one year due to production difficulties, but the quality is exactly what you'd expect from our publishing house. You can order now at—" He paused to remember, then rattled off a long, complicated URL that no one would be able to remember.

Howard added, "It should be at the bottom of your screen."

I was growing impatient. "The important thing is that the *Necronomicon* has been stolen! Someone broke into the publishing offices and snatched it away. If you have any information on the whereabouts of this book, please contact Howard Phillips Publishing. I've been hired as a consultant to help them locate the lost object."

Dick couldn't turn his head on the china platter, but his eyes flicked back and forth until his gaze landed on me again.

"Tell us the entire story, Dan-O, all the juicy details—or do we have to wait to read about it in the next adventure?"

Before I could answer, Dick saw the cameraman raise two fingers, then he cut me off. "That's all the time we have for today! Thank you, gentlemen, for this entertaining and in-depth interview. And now for a word from our sponsors."

The red lights above the cameras winked off, and Dick the Head laughed. "That was excellent, Dan-O. Once we see the ratings, we may want you on again—next time with Robin."

I couldn't see what we had accomplished. "Did we talk enough about the crime? I'm not sure how this helped."

"We got publicity," Philip said.

The goblin makeup artist offered us each a packet of moist towelettes to smear away the face powder.

"Publicity is how we'll flush out the thief," said Howard. "And increase sales. We'll get a flood of orders for the new *Necronomicon* now and also move the backstock of the Shamble & Die series."

"I thought all those books were burned in the bonfire," I said.

"We'll do a new overprinting," Philip said, "then liquidate the extra copies."

CHAPTER 32

After the long day, with doppelganger threats and a stolen *Necronomicon*, I vowed not to miss my scheduled appointment at Bruno & Heinrich's Embalming Parlor. I definitely needed some freshening up.

Because I work on so many stressful and potentially apocalyptic cases, I had to stay in tip-top shape, at the peak of my mental abilities. When trying to solve mysteries, I like to mull over facts, suspicions, and contradictions until I can put things together. The embalming parlor served a dual purpose, much-needed personal care and a good environment for a brainstorm.

After the Big Uneasy, Bruno and Heinrich had turned a previously unrecognized niche market into a thriving business. The two proprietors had built up a clientele of discerning undead customers who refused to give in to decay.

Right now, my joints needed a little silicone and grease, and my skin deserved a touch-up of formaldehyde. I usually didn't bother with the fancy flourishes, although Sheyenne sometimes booked me for a manicure.

Heinrich and his brother were humans, but they looked cadaverously gaunt, as if they practiced embalming techniques on each other before offering them to customers. The two were also twins—another set, and I was already seeing double everywhere—with slicked-back dark hair. Heinrich drew heavy mascara around his left eye, while Bruno applied the mascara around both eyes. They painted their fingernails black.

Trained as morticians, the pair really wanted to be makeup artists, but could not achieve that dream due to lack of human interpersonal skills. When zombies like me returned to the world, however, Heinrich and Bruno had discovered the perfect balance. They could hold snappy conversations with the undead, and they laughed at their customers' comebacks, no matter how slow or slurred they might sound.

"Felicitations, Mr. Shamble!" said Heinrich, holding the shop door open for me. "We haven't seen you in some time. You must be in need of a top off." When Bruno joined him, I differentiated the two by paying close attention to the mascara.

I removed my fedora. "I've been staying fresh enough with a monthly maintenance spell from Mavis and Alma Wannovich."

Bruno's face tightened. "Oh, poo poo on that. Come to us for truly artisanal embalming."

Heinrich seized my left hand, ran his thumb along my cuticles. "Tsk-tsk, the condition of these nails! You look as if you've just clawed yourself out of a grave."

"That was quite a few years ago," I said, "but I've had some hard cases in the meantime."

"And what about lotions?" Bruno asked. "Do you use lotions?"

Henrich agreed. "It rubs the lotion on its skin."

"Not often enough," I admitted, looking to the back room of the parlor. "Is my private chair ready? I have some cases to ruminate."

"Indeed, Mr. Shamble," Heinrich said. "We call our privacy suite the ruminating room, as we refresh your bodily systems."

In the front parlor, three sallow litches sat in chairs lined up before a row of mirrors, where they stared at their ghastly faces. One of the junior embalming techs flared eyeshadow and charcoal dust to add sunken tones to their cheeks, then teased out new tangles in their hair. A middle-aged zombie man reclined in his own chair, snoring loudly as embalming fluid was pumped into him.

The ruminating room in back had a single chair, mood lighting, and a privacy screen. I took my place and tried to relax as Heinrich tended me. The morbidly loquacious embalmer kept chattering about how he would leave me alone to think, while he hooked up the tubes and pumps. I couldn't get a word in edgewise.

Seeing these twins reminded me of Mavis's fears of doppelgangers. Mentally, I reviewed Hairy Harry's restored normal neighborhood, and Mary Celeste's Elm Street, and they did indeed seem too good to be true, like somebody's nostalgic dream. McGoo's personality had also changed—quiet, clean, professional. His career and his marriage would have been well served if he'd learned how to keep his mouth shut more often, instead of putting his foot in it. But this new calm and collected McGoo was not the same as my best friend.

Heinrich started a refreshing course of fluid into my blood vessels. As he droned on, I couldn't concentrate on the tangled mysteries, so I took a different approach and decided to use him as a sounding board.

"You're human, Heinrich, but you and your brother fit in quite well here in the Quarter. Does it ever bother you not to have the world back the way it was?"

"Normal, you mean?" Heinrich let out a nervous little laugh. "No, no, no, not at all! Even before the Big Uneasy I was a little bit unnatural myself. Now, Bruno and I fit in much better. We have learned how to balance our lives."

"What if the Big Uneasy had never happened? Or what if it were reversed now?"

"Why, then all of our customers would go away!" Heinrich said, horrified. "And that would be bad for business."

"It would be bad for unnaturals in a lot of ways," I said.

The mortician adjusted the pump output, and I felt rejuvenated as fresh fluid entered all the right places.

Heinrich ran a black-nailed finger along his lower lip as he mused. "Well, if the Big Uneasy had never happened at all, then I would be an unhappy, albeit successful, mortician. Now that people don't always stay dead, Bruno and I have repeat customers—like yourself." He gave me a wide, corpse-like smile. "And how would it change for you, Mr. Shamble? You would most certainly still be a detective—it's what you are." He chuckled again. "It's in your blood … or in your fluids."

"Well, my caseload would've come to an end when this happened." I tapped the hole in my forehead. "End of story."

Heinrich hummed as he opened his extensive makeup kit and fussed with my face. "Always look on the bright side of life and death." He took out white sponge wedges, dampened a cloth. He spritzed cool water on my face and began to apply himself to the task. "My, my, my, this powder is hideous. Why would you choose a flesh tone for your complexion?"

"It was for my TV interview with Dick the Head," I said. "A makeup error."

He hummed in disapproval. "I'm disappointed you didn't come for your touch-up before the TV interview. You should have looked your best for such a prominent appearance."

"Dick the Head stole the show. He wants to be the best-looking zombie face on the stage."

The mortician sniffed. "Now, that one could use some work, if you ask my opinion." He continued to apply the sponges. "There, unnatural *au naturel.*" Heinrich used a fine scraping tool to clean the edges of the bullet hole, but I told him not to bother with the mortician's putty, since it never stayed in place anyway.

He disconnected the last tubes, then brushed my hair, making sure every strand was in the right place, then cemented the style with a liberal dose of hairspray. When it hardened, he replaced my fedora where it belonged.

"There, Mr. Chambeaux! You are ready for the Unnatural Quarter again."

CHAPTER 33

When I got back to the office, fresh from the embalming parlor, I was both relieved and a little disappointed that no one had actually watched *Conversations with Dick the Head* that afternoon. Robin and Alvina were busy with other distractions, and Sheyenne glowed bright with her own news. "This is exciting, Beaux—just what we've been waiting for!"

"All of our clients paid their bills?" I asked.

"Even better! Wrex's Auto Repair called—the Pro Bono Mobile is done, good as new."

I'd never seen the car when it was new, or even when Robin had first bought it, but I'd be happy to have it running again, considering its previous disassembled state.

She drifted next to me. "Let's go pick it up right away—I'll come with you."

Robin emerged from her office, retrieved two folders from the tall file cabinet, and retreated to her desk. She looked very relieved to hear about the car.

Busy posting a new blog at her table, Alvina waved to me. "I'll answer the phones while you're away."

Sheyenne smiled. "I'm training her in office duties. Even if she'll always look ten years old, she's going to need to have business skills."

After returning from WRIP, I'd pulled the hearse around

the corner to find a big enough space. "I enjoyed the fancy loaner, but the Pro Bono Mobile is easier to park."

Drifting into the passenger seat, Sheyenne buckled her seat belt out of habit, even though the worst fender bender wouldn't damage her ectoplasmic self. I wrapped my stiff fingers around the hearse's steering wheel and enjoyed driving it for the last time. But the Pro Bono Mobile was our trademark, so long as the engine was running.

I headed for the auto repair shop. Seeing the hearse pass by, a seedy-looking vampire stuck out his thumb for a ride, but we were going the other direction.

I parked the loaner in the rear of Wrex's Auto Repair, and I was relieved to see the lime-green, rust-spattered Maverick in the side lot, ready to go. It didn't look as good as new, but it looked as good as always.

As we headed for the office, Towin' Owen rumbled up with a pile of scrap metal and crumpled auto parts, shattered windshield panels, dangling mirrors, broken exhaust pipes. The ogre grinned at us as he climbed out of the cab. "Big pileup on the freeway, and it's like a treasure hunt. Could be worth something." He raised the bed of his tow truck and, with a noise like a dozen drum kits dropping from the sky, he dumped the twisted metal onto the cracked asphalt.

Sheyenne and I entered the main office, where Wrex sat on his stool, toying with the car keys in the bowl. From the back, we could hear the usual bangs, whirs, and dropped tools in the repair bay. When the gremlin saw us, he snagged the familiar Ford key. "As promised, your vehicle is repaired and improved."

"Improved? We didn't request that," Sheyenne said.

"What did you improve?" I asked, worried that Robin would be upset.

With a sly look, the gremlin whispered, "You'll see. A little fine-tuning here and there, upgraded parts, performance fuel, a fresh coat of paint. Fully Wrexed!"

Sheyenne grew serious. "Our enhanced service agreement covers all the charges?"

"Oh, the vehicle has a lot of charge now! Real pep, if you need it." Wrex grabbed a pen out of a cup so he could check boxes on a form. "We'll submit everything to the insurance company." He thrust the clipboard at me. "Just sign here to verify that you authorized all those improvements."

"But I didn't," I said.

"Oh, yes you did." The gremlin tapped the fine print on the bottom of the form. "You authorized repairs 'as needed.' And in my expert opinion, you needed a lot of repairs."

"I just don't want to get shafted," I warned.

Wrex took it as a compliment. "Yes, we included new shafts."

Sheyenne didn't seem overly bothered. "That's why we paid for the premium plan, Beaux. There should be no questions asked."

"But I'm a zombie detective. I ask a lot of questions."

Wrex extended the keys. "Take her for a spin. Our repairs are guaranteed."

Outside, we walked around the Pro Bono Mobile, inspected the body, the tires. I lifted the hood and bent over to look knowledgeably at the engine, though I knew nothing about cars. I gave a satisfied nod. When I slammed the hood back down, rust flakes pattered onto the asphalt.

"Just like the Pro Bono Mobile," Sheyenne said.

Wrex stood against the wall, watching. "But better. Ah, so much better!"

With trepidation and anticipation I opened the door, glad

to hear the familiar groan. I settled into the worn seat, inserted the key into the ignition.

Outside, Sheyenne drifted above the front bumper like a cheerleader.

I turned the key, and the engine coughed, rumbled, then started up with a satisfyingly loud roar. I eased off on the gas and let the engine idle, but the noise dissipated only a little.

Wrex watched with pride. I leaned out the window and shouted, "The muffler sounds awfully loud! And the engine!"

"Yes, powerful!" The gremlin rubbed his clawed hands together. "We installed extra volume."

"I guess we aren't going to use the car for any quiet stake-outs or stealthy operations," I said.

A gleam came to the gremlin's eyes. "My guys could upgrade and install stealth mode for an extra fifty dollars."

Sheyenne took her place in the passenger seat. "We'll test the car first. Exactly what improvements did you include, and how do we access them?"

The phone rang inside the office, and Wrex scuttled back to answer it. "Don't worry, you'll find out!"

In front of the repair shop, next to Towin' Owen's pile of twisted and wrecked parts, Winkin, Blinkin, and Todd formed a fireman's brigade to move all the fresh debris into the repair bays.

The Pro Bono Mobile kept purring at maximum volume. Bracing myself, I glanced into the rearview mirror, eased the car into reverse, and backed up. I took it slow, just to make sure, but soon we were out on the road, driving along.

Although the rumble of the Maverick's engine stifled all conversation, it felt like cruising with my ghost girlfriend. The drive was short but sweet, and I let myself feel satisfied, not concerned with cases ... though I was still worried about the threat of doppelgangers and overly normalized neighborhoods.

When I approached our office building, I spotted Linda Bullwer lurking by a tree, trying to hide in its shade as she kept spying. I let out an exasperated sigh. "She must be staking out our offices, taking notes."

When she heard the Pro Bono Mobile—probably a block before we came into view—the vampire ghostwriter crouched behind the tree, where she could observe us. I glared at her, and when our eyes met, she darted away.

I'd had my fill of paranoia for the day. Linda had been slinking around the Goblin Tavern, lurking in the Ghoul's Diner, watching Mary Celeste's street, snooping into the re-inhabited (by doppelgangers?) neighborhoods, and now she was loitering outside our office building.

"I'm going to get to the bottom of this, Spooky—the rock bottom," I said, determined. "All this paranoia is making me nervous."

"As paranoia usually does," she said.

But according to the old adage, it's not paranoia if someone really is watching you, and Linda Bullwer was spying on me. I was sure of that.

CHAPTER 34

With the Maverick coughing out exhaust fumes from the noise-enhanced muffler, I dropped off Sheyenne (who didn't even need to open the door). As she flitted off, I accelerated away like a drag-racing contender. I circled the block, and when I came up behind the furtive ghostwriter, the brakes squealed—another part that had been restored to its previous level of poor functionality.

Even so, I somehow managed to startle her. I leaned out the window. "You keep watching me, Linda, so I must be doing something interesting. Better tell me what it is."

Though skittish, she managed an indignant, and false, huff. "It's a public street, Mr. Shamble, and you're a public figure, since my stories have made you famous."

I tried a different approach—direct accusation. "Why are you spying on me? Why not just ask what you want? I've always been willing to answer your questions."

"Because I ... because I don't know if you're one of them!" She pushed her cat's-eye glasses up on her nose. "Or two of them."

Doppelgangers again.

"Everybody keeps seeing double." I had to raise my voice over the loud engine.

She stepped a little closer to the driver's side window. "I

need to speak with you in private." Her pale vampire skin went even paler. "Extremely private, where no one can hear us." She glanced over her shoulder at the usual unnatural pedestrian traffic. "This could be your biggest case ever. I have to tell you what I know—but no eavesdroppers! It could be dangerous."

I decided to go back to the library. "Get in. I know just the place."

She went around the car and climbed in. Uneasy, we chose not to speak to each other, not that we could hear over the engine. When I pulled up in front of the imposing main branch, I claimed a one-hour parking spot designated for "readers of short books only." The noise of the Pro Bono Mobile made the guardian stone lions frown at us.

Linda seemed uneasy wherever she went. "Let's get inside, if you're sure we can find a private place—I don't like to be out in the open. People can see us, hear us … maybe snatch us and duplicate us."

With remarkable speed, she scurried up the steps, and I lurched after her. The stone lions rose up to challenge us for our library cards, but Linda's cross expression cowed them enough to let us pass. I think they were just happy that I'd shut off the Maverick's loud engine.

Inside the echoing mausoleum of books, students sat at long tables poring over dusty tomes. At the back of the main gallery, a clot of worn beanbag chairs formed a reading circle. Several orc children snarled with laughter as a volunteer librarian read aloud from an orc children's tale filled with blood and mayhem.

I went bravely up to the dreaded reference desk, where Frieda sat with her hair in a prim bun, squinting through over-sized glasses. Her multiple articulated limbs flurried in a complex dance of rearranging returned books on her cart. She hissed when she saw me. "Back again! I can see the guilt on your face. Do you have a late book to return?"

I touched my cheek, finding only a leftover smear of makeup from the WRIP studio. "No, ma'am. We'd like to use the Cone of Silence, please, for a private discussion."

Linda Bullwer joined me. "A very private discussion, and we need a very silent cone where no one can overhear us."

Frieda clucked in disapproval. "The Cone of Silence is not a place where people should talk. That defeats the purpose."

"It's a discussion about a book," I suggested, hoping that might do the trick.

"That's a better answer," the Spider Lady admitted. "Unfortunately, the room is reserved for the entire day. Two patrons are doing a binge read of the Shamble & Die series, and their laughter is so loud it disturbed the other customers. But I didn't want to discourage them from reading, so the Cone of Silence was the best solution. I'm afraid I can't help you."

"What are we going to do?" Linda groaned in dismay. "We need a place to talk, Mr. Shamble, and we mustn't be overheard. This is urgent!"

Then the obvious solution occurred to me. "I always have a Plan B. There's another place no one will overhear us." I should have thought of it earlier.

Back in the Pro Bono Mobile, I started the engine and clicked the door lock. The roar and the rumble rattled the windows.

"Where are we going now?" Linda asked, growing more and more tense.

"Staying right here." I had to raise my voice. "With this engine, nobody can hear a word we're saying. We'll be drowned out."

"What?" she asked. I tried again, and this time she understood. "Oh, I agree! Our conversation will be safe and secure." The exhaust backfired. The engine rumbled and idled, like a large ogre badly in need of decongestant.

Now I was the impatient one. "This has gone on long enough, Miss Bullwer. Fill me in before anything happens to either of us."

Her eyes widened. "You think they're after us now?"

"I don't even know who you're worried about. Tell me."

She screwed up her courage. "After writing all of those complex detective mysteries, I've become a pretty good sleuth myself. I'm attuned to questions that don't have the right kind of answers. While doing research for the *Necronomicon* sequel, I've also been taking notes for the next Shamble & Die novel. I think there may be a truly diabolical plot afoot."

"I've been keeping my eye on the Olde Tymers," I said. "Those troublemakers tried to kidnap Stella Artois right from the front of the library." I looked around, but saw no sign of the psychedelic Scooby van following us. "They also caused a ruckus burning books at Howard Phillips Publishing."

Linda pinched her cat's-eye glasses and nodded. "The protest may have been a diversion so that someone could steal the *Necronomicon*." She leaned closer and muttered words that were entirely drowned out by the engine noise. Frustrated, she tried again, and finally stopped whispering. "I don't believe the book was stolen by a mere collector—there's a much darker purpose, perhaps an attempt to unravel the Big Uneasy."

"The Olde Tymers tried to do the same thing by abducting Stella, but they didn't really have a plan."

Linda remained skittish. "Yes, that librarian is the key! Don't underestimate her. I am convinced that she is involved somehow—maybe even the ringleader behind the nefarious plan."

"But what is the nefarious plan?"

The engine backfired again, and the gunshot sound was enough to startle the ghostwriter. "That's all I can say!" Linda popped open the door and bolted away.

CHAPTER 35

I mulled over what I had learned … which wasn't much. On my way back to the offices, I made up my mind to call McGoo. Maybe I could put him under a bright light and demand to know if he was a doppelganger. I would throw stupid jokes at him and watch how he responded. That would prove whether he was really my friend or some bad photocopy.

It was the only way to be sure.

Or maybe Alvina and I could sneak over to his small, cluttered apartment and search the closet and under the bed for body-snatcher pods.…

Robin came out of her office, flipping through folders and shaking her head as she studied columns of names. "I'm trying to put together a class-action suit, but each of these missing persons from Elm Street insists that they are no longer missing. That puts an end to our case."

Sheyenne let out a ghostly sigh. "So much for paying the bills."

Robin remained determined, though. "I'm going to keep tracing the formerly missing people, and I've already got most of the inhabitants on Hairy Harry's street. I don't like loose ends."

The Wannoviches entered our offices on tiptoe and tip-hoof, still ultracautious from their paranoia. Mavis carried an armload of books, and Alma had a pack with even more volumes wrapped around her spotted back. "We've made some progress, Mr. Shamble. I think we found a solution."

Alvina ran over to hug the sow.

"Progress is always a step in the right direction," I said.

"We studied all the duplication magic in our book catalog," Mavis said. "Howard Phillips used to publish an entire line of copycat spells, but then too many cats were copied, and animal control had to be called."

Alvina unbuckled the pack and carried the sow's books to the homework table, while Mavis dropped the heaviest tome next to the kid's *Make My Day* marketing plan.

"Is there a market for copycat spells?" I asked.

Bending over, Mavis began turning the yellowed pages in the main tome. She pushed her pointy hat out of the way. "Lots of people like to clone themselves so they can get more things done. Better known as the 'If only there could be two of me!' syndrome. Some people want to make a better version of themselves, while others like to have a placeholder doppelganger to punch a timeclock, so the real person can be off doing fun activities."

"That's cheating," Robin said.

"If they're identical, how can you tell which is the real one?" I asked. "Is there a barcode to show that someone's a doppelganger instead of the real person?"

"It depends on the spell method." With her long fingernails, Mavis flipped pages until she found the spell in question. "This one's a classic."

The sow circled the table, snuffling the floor, where she found a few crumbs of red velvet cake.

Sheyenne drifted closer, concerned. "These spell books should be restricted. Can anyone just use these incantations?"

"We have the only spare copies of the books," Mavis said. "Howard and Philip keep their collection under tight security."

I snorted. "Yeah, just like they kept the *Necronomicon* safe."

"That was an exception," Mavis said. "The only other place you'd find this spell book would be in the main branch of the UQ library, in their special rare tomes collection."

I tried to read the spell on the yellowed pages, but it was written in a language I didn't understand. "I'm not fluent in magical nonsense."

Mavis's black dress rustled as she took a seat in the chair. "Alma and I will help you find the body-snatching culprit. See here." She pointed to more gibberish. "It's crosslinked with a Stepford neighborhood spell."

Now things started to make sense. The people from Elm Street and Hairy Harry's neighbors certainly did have a Stepford vibe. I couldn't help thinking about the changed version of McGoo. "But how do we get the real ones back? That's the most important thing."

Mavis adjusted her wide-brimmed hat. "The doppelganger spell makes echoes, copies—and the real person is bottled up somewhere else." She raised her finger. "So you see, the answer is obvious."

"I'm sure it is," I said, waiting for her to make it more obvious.

"The real person is *bottled up* somewhere." She paused again, waiting, then continued in greater detail. "Therefore, you need a magic bottle opener!"

With a sound of clanking metal, she rummaged in her voluminous black satchel and pulled out a small implement and held it up with a triumphant flourish. "A bottle opener! A churchkey—which makes it even more holy." Her big grin showed off her snaggly teeth.

The churchkey's opening was wide enough to fit over any standard bottlecap. Runes were etched along the metal handle.

"This magic churchkey is inscribed with spells. Now, hold the runes like so." She extended the bottle opener straight out in front of her. "Then make this motion with your wrist." She flicked her hand, as if popping open an invisible bottle of beer. "And you must say the magic sound—*fsshhht-ahhhhh!* And *voila!* A magic bottle opener. I practiced the spell myself."

I took the churchkey and turned it over in my hand. "So, I use this on one of the duplicates? I find a doppelganger and make the bottle-opening motion?"

Mavis nodded. "And say the spell, *fsshhht-ahhhhh!*"

I practiced. "Can this be used more than once? There may be a lot of doppelgangers in the Quarter."

"It should be good for several uses, at least three or four."

I thought of all the people on Elm Street, all of Hairy Harry's neighbors. And McGoo. For starters.

"We're going to need a lot more than this."

Mavis jangled in her black satchel and pulled out a handful of identical churchkeys. "I had them mass produced. If we hand them out, then others can help us erase the doppelgangers. I'll rest more easily once I know the bottled-up people are released."

Alvina said, "I think there's something wrong with my other half-daddy."

"I think so, too, kid." I stuffed my jacket pockets with the magical churchkeys, ready to go in search of bad copies. My first priority was to track down McGoo, but when I called he didn't answer his phone. Unfortunately, this new version of my best human friend took his job seriously and didn't accept personal phone calls during work hours.

The first place I decided to look was at Mary Celeste's

neighborhood, which was already back to "normal," but likely filled with doppelgangers. If nothing else, I could make sure Mary was all right, and she could lend me a hand. Or four.

WHEN I RUSHED BACK TO ELM STREET, NOTHING HAD CHANGED since my last visit. The lizard demon was still washing his car, the werewolf boy was still riding his bicycle with training wheels, while his father and older brother still played catch.

I knocked on the door of Mary's townhouse, but when she didn't answer, I guessed she might be at work. As I was about to turn away, though, the door creaked open and the ambipolydextrous young woman looked at me with a frighteningly bland expression. "May I help you?"

My flesh crawled. "Mary, don't you know me?"

"Yes, Mr. Shamble," she said in a monotone. "I didn't expect to see you again, now that the case is solved. We're all fine on Elm Street, everything back to normal. There's nothing more for you to do here." She tried to close the door in my face.

"We'll see about that," I said.

Time for my first practice spell, and I knew I'd need to use it many times before the job was done. I pulled out one of the magic churchkeys and held it in front of me, as Mavis had shown me.

Mary showed no interest as I flicked my wrist and made the potent bottle-opening sound. *"Fsshhht-ahhhhh!"*

The air sparkled around Mary, and she suddenly shuddered. Her hands twitched, her arms flailed, and she clutched her heart with two hands and her gut with the other two.

"Oh!" She straightened and extended her palms in front of

her, amazed. Her expression became wild and startled, and her eyes had a new light. "What happened? Where was I?"

"What do you remember? Just yesterday I saw you washing dishes at the diner. You got into a fight with Esther the waitress, so I know you were really *you*. But just now ..."

The multi-limbed girl shook her head. "I was in a very strange place, like a surreal miniaturized version of my neighborhood." She peered down the street, looked at the houses, the neighbors, the sidewalk. "It wasn't like this at all."

"They've all been bottled up, but I just released you. These people aren't real—they're doppelgangers."

Mary put all four hands on her hips, overlapping palms. "How can we help them? I want my real neighborhood back."

"It's an easy spell—otherwise, I wouldn't remember it myself." I withdrew four more churchkeys from my jacket pocket. "Here's how you do it." I demonstrated the magical bottle opening, made the potent sound.

Mary took a churchkey in each of her hands. "Let's go—one at a time, up and down the street."

I pulled out another bottle opener for myself. Mary moved so fast I had to shamble at top speed to keep up with her.

The little werewolf boy wobbled toward us on his bicycle. Mary pointed the bottle opener at him, popped it in the air, and said, *"Fsshhht-ahhhhh!"* The boy shuddered, and his bicycle toppled over, despite the training wheels. The little werewolf began to howl.

"Now, that's more like the street I remember," Mary said. "I'm going to make sure everyone is restored from whoever body-snatched them. I'll show them what normal is really supposed to be like."

I still felt uneasy and anxious about McGoo. "I'll let you take care of this, Mary. I have to find my best friend."

Mary was on a mission. With her four hands and her determination, no doubt she'd have all the doppelgangers gone from Elm Street in no time.

I hurried off on my next place to look for McGoo: Hairy Harry's neighborhood.

CHAPTER 36

At his first opportunity, my best human friend had exhibited clear signs of hero worship toward the legendary werewolf cop, but he had not been the same after he'd come back from Hairy Harry's neighborhood. Maybe, though, his doppelganger would have wandered back to the scene of the duplicating.

With more magic churchkeys in my pocket, I was a zombie on a mission.

When I approached Hairy Harry's house, I hoped to hear the hellhound baying—which would at least be an indication of something normal. Real normal, rather than abnormal normal. But I didn't hear so much as a yip.

Lucky was curled up on the lawn, his spiked chain anchored to the steel post in the ground. When I came up the driveway, the beast opened his blazing red eyes and let out a congenial woof from lungs the size of blacksmith's bellows. But that was all.

The werewolf cop still sat on his front porch, drinking a can of beer and watching another baseball game on the portable TV.

I was surprised and relieved to find McGoo sitting next to him in a second lawn chair with a box of doughnuts on his lap. He raised a doughnut in salute. "Hey, Shamble." He took a bite, spilling powdered sugar on the front of his uniform.

"Aren't you supposed to be on your rounds?" I asked.

"I'm eating doughnuts, which is also a traditional cop duty."

Lucky rose to his paws and shook himself. His spiked collar rattled back and forth, and the chain actually fell off the post. Hairy Harry hadn't even secured it.

The werewolf cop took another swig of beer and lounged back, barely acknowledging me. "We're watching the baseball game."

"And eating doughnuts," McGoo added.

I muttered under my breath, "I'll sure be glad to have the real you back, McGoo." I pulled a magic bottle opener from my pocket and extended the churchkey to work the spell. "Time to un-doppel you."

But just as I twitched my wrist and made the incantation sound, Lucky ambled in front of me.

As soon as I said *Fsshhht-ahhhhh!* the spiraling magic struck the huge hellhound instead of McGoo or Hairy Harry. I had not intended to restore Lucky, at least not yet, but suddenly the slavering beast became true to his namesake. The rambunctious puppy energy was no longer bottled up inside him, but released like a furiously shaken can of beer.

Lucky's roaring bark was loud enough to topple the mailbox at the end of the driveway.

I dug into my pocket to grab another magic churchkey. Before things got out of hand, I needed to restore the real Hairy Harry! He was the only one who could control his service hellhound.

I pulled out another handful of the magical tools, but before I could raise the bottle opener, Lucky planted his massive paws on my chest and bowled me over backward. The churchkeys clattered out of my hands.

Now, the hellhound let out a decidedly unfriendly snarl. His scarlet eyes blazed.

I rolled aside and scrambled to my feet, dodging. As I dashed to the side of the house, the hellhound bounded after me, barking and snarling. I tripped over the rusted downspout, then crashed into the hedge line as I headed for the backyard.

The neighbors didn't even look up. Nobody offered to help. Nobody complained about the ruckus. An amphibious creature was watering his flowerbed next door, and he just looked at me as I bounded past him with the hellhound hot on my tail.

Behind Hairy's house, I vaulted over a splintered picnic table into the fenced backyard, knocked over a stack of plastic tubs. When I glanced over my shoulder, I stepped in something big, brown, and soft—and I could guess what Lucky had left in the lawn. I kept running.

The hellhound crashed through a thorn hedge, uprooting the bushes. He was playing with me, I think, or maybe he really did want to devour me. Heinrich and Bruno had assured me that their embalming chemicals left no aftertaste.

I turned the corner on the far side of the backyard and headed around the house, up the other hedge line, to the front again. I needed another chance with the magic bottle opener.

McGoo was still eating a doughnut in the lawn chair. Hairy Harry had turned his attention back to the ballgame, as if they had forgotten about me.

When Lucky galloped to the front porch, the werewolf cop looked up. "Good doggie."

That diverted the hellhound's attention for just a second, but it was enough. I dropped to my knees and scrabbled in the patchy crabgrass. I grabbed one of the magic bottle openers, pointed it at McGoo, and went through the motions. *"Fsshhht-ahhhhh!"*

This time, the de-doppel spell slammed into my best human friend. McGoo shook his head, stared in confusion at the box of doughnuts on his lap and the powdered sugar on his fingers. "What the—?"

"McGoo, I need your help!"

My shout only attracted the hellhound's attention. Lucky let out a monstrous howl.

McGoo noticed the werewolf cop on the lawn chair next to him. "Hey, you're Hairy Harry! In person!"

The dog bowled me over again, but I did manage to grab one more churchkey from the grass. Even as the nightmarish puppy rolled with me on the lawn, I was able to pop open the bottled-up real version of Hairy Harry.

The magic seemed to take forever, but the surly werewolf finally lurched out of his rickety chair. "Shamble, what are you doing here? Leave my dog alone!"

"Help!"

Thinking fast, McGoo tossed a doughnut toward Lucky. "Here, boy! Have a cruller." He threw another one, a jelly doughnut, which splattered the hellhound's fur with gooey red jam.

The restored Hairy Harry strode toward his service animal. "Get off of him, boy." With a clawed hand, he seized the spiked collar and wrestled the enormous hellhound back. "Sorry, Shamble. He gets a little frisky."

Rumpled and slightly damaged, I climbed back to my feet and looked at the confused men in front of me. "I meant to release you two first, but Lucky got in the way."

"Lucky always gets in the way." With his free paw, Hairy Harry scratched behind the hound's ears.

McGoo was still baffled. "Where was I? I remember a very weird place, like a funhouse-mirror version of the Quarter."

Even as the hellhound struggled against the chain, Hairy Harry dug his heels into the lawn and yanked on the choke collar. "Stay, Lucky! Stay! Good boy."

The beast let out a bellowing howl that cracked nearby windows.

Next door, the amphibious creature continued watering his flowerbed, unconcerned.

The werewolf cop snarled at me and McGoo. "Help me drag him to his kennel in back. He won't like it, but he's got to learn to behave. Lucky's supposed to be my service dog, and now he's given me PTSD all over again."

The three of us managed to heave and haul the hellhound into his kennel, a barred enclosure the size of a bomb shelter. As expected, he whined, miserable and forlorn. But we had another emergency on our hands.

When we got back to the front porch, Hairy Harry slumped into his lawn chair. "I'll have one of those doughnuts, Officer McGoohan. To go with my beer."

McGoo offered him the box, and then the werewolf cop turned his predatory gaze toward me. "Now, punk, you better explain what the hell is going on here."

CHAPTER 37

Supervillains like to give lengthy soliloquies of their dastardly plans, but detectives are good at explanations, too, once they've solved a case. It's part of the job.

While Lucky offered canine commentary from his kennel, I talked about the vanished and swapped neighborhoods, the bad copies and the bottled-up real personalities. And the magic churchkeys that Mavis and Alma had created.

Hairy Harry's fur bristled as he listened, but McGoo wasn't as convinced. "That's only a half-solved case, Shamble. You don't even know who's doing it or why! Don't go taking a victory lap yet."

"Half solved is better than nothing, and I'm still investigating. Now that you're restored as my sidekick, we can track down the culprit. And de-doppel all these people."

"Who's a sidekick?" McGoo huffed.

"Just semantics," I said, not wanting to belabor the obvious. "We can't waste any time. I've already restored Mary Celeste and gave her a spare set of magic churchkeys. She's busy unbottling all of Elm Street."

As the hellhound continued to whimper in his kennel, Hairy Harry scanned the street full of doppelganger residents. He didn't sound entirely happy. "I suppose we have to restore this neighborhood, too." He let out a deep rumbling sigh. "Back the way it was."

On the portable television, a batter hit a home run, and the crowd roared. The werewolf cop cursed and changed the channel. "Losers! Time for my favorite talk show anyway." He tuned in WRIP just as the catchy opening music came up for *Conversations with Dick the Head*. "He always has interesting guests. I was in a daze, though ... can't even remember who was on the past couple of days."

"You missed a really good one yesterday," I said.

When the picture became staticky, he swatted the side of the old television with his paw, and the image miraculously sharpened.

Resting on his china serving platter, Dick the Head greeted his audience. When the TV was drowned out by a loud car engine, I turned to see the lime-green Pro Bono Mobile prowl down the street and pull up in front of Hairy Harry's house. Robin was behind the wheel, so I knew it must be an emergency.

Although the werewolf cop was more interested in the talk show, McGoo rose to his feet and set the box of doughnuts on the lawn chair.

Robin jumped out of the car, armed for battle with her briefcase. "Dan, I thought you might be here! Good news— we're getting calls from the Elm Street residents! Now that Mary has restored them, they may want to file a class-action lawsuit after all."

"Not the good news I was expecting, but it'll do."

"We have a problem with the paperwork, though," she cautioned. "We can't demand damages until we know who's to blame."

"Working on that," I said. "We'll have more witnesses as

soon as we use the bottle openers and restore Hairy Harry's neighborhood."

McGoo brushed powdered sugar from his uniform. "That only helps if anybody remembers something. I sure don't."

Robin gave him a skeptical assessment. "Are you the real Toby McGoohan, or are you a doppelganger?"

By way of an answer, he looked to me. "Hey, Shamble, what's the only room in the house where you're safe from zombies?"

I didn't understand what he was doing. "What does that have to do with anything?"

"The living room!" He laughed.

Thus, I knew it was my real best friend.

Robin didn't dignify the joke with a laugh, but she accepted it as proof.

We all turned our attention to the portable television as Dick the Head introduced his guests—a tall man with mutton-chop sideburns and a prim woman in corset and frilly blouse, the first Olde Tymers we had seen at the *Necronomicon* launch gala.

Dick the Head forced the joke. "Today is Throwback Thursday in a big way! We'll be talking with some humans who claim the world was wonderful even without unnaturals. Ha! I might take issue with that."

"Not just wonderful," said the man, "but *normal*."

The disembodied head's lips turned down in a scowl. "This is Mr. Rupert Gleens, president and chairman of the Olde Tymers Society. And his wife, Violet." Her dress was clearly lavender, or perhaps periwinkle, depending on how clear Hairy Harry's reception was.

"My actual title is 'head' of the Olde Tymers Society,"

Rupert said, trying to be friendly with the host. "See, we're both *heads.*"

The old-fashioned woman pouted behind her granny spectacles. "To be clear, we don't have a *problem* with unnaturals, so long as they stay in their place." She sniffed. "And that place is nonexistence."

"Glad you have such an open mind," said Dick.

"Some of my best friends are unnaturals," said Rupert.

"Remember G-O-D," Violet added.

Robin turned from the TV, and I could see her blood was beginning to boil. "Are those the same people who tried to abduct poor Stella Artois?"

"No witnesses could identify them," I said.

McGoo scratched his head. "I remember filing an arrest warrant after the attempted kidnapping … but I left some of the parts blank."

"You weren't yourself at the time, McGoo," I said.

Robin looked concerned. "You know, we haven't heard from Stella after you gave her the signature pages a few days ago. I hope she's all right—she certainly has enough home security."

I remembered the vampire ghostwriter's strange conspiracy theories. "Linda Bullwer told me some crackpot idea that Stella herself might be connected with the disappearances, reappearances, and renormalizations."

Robin pondered the idea. "Sometimes, crackpot theories are our best hope."

On TV, Rupert and Violet Gleens drew our immediate attention as their voices rose in anger. The two rambled into painfully distorted memories of life before the Big Uneasy. "Everything has changed," Violet whined. "We can't raise our kids in a normal environment."

Dick the Head brightened. "Oh, do you have kids?"

"No," Rupert said, "but we can make decisions for other people's kids."

"Tell us about the Olde Tymers Society. What exactly would you like to accomplish?"

"We want to erase the Big Uneasy!" Violet said. "Undo it. Send the unnaturals back to where they belong."

Dick frowned. "My guest yesterday gave us an exclusive scoop that the original *Necronomicon* had been stolen. Was your little group behind that crime?"

"Of course not!" said an indignant Rupert.

"We would never steal," Violet added.

"Apparently kidnapping is okay, though," I muttered to the TV.

Rupert continued, leaning closer to the head. "The *Necronomicon* contains powerful magic, and therefore it's the key to restoring our proud country. But since the book has vanished, we have to direct our anger and retribution in a more productive direction."

"And what is that?" asked Dick the Head, as if he really wanted to know.

"Vengeance on the person responsible for this debacle!"

Violet Gleens nodded. "The librarian Stella Artois! Spilling her virgin's blood might have been an accident, but that doesn't mean we don't want revenge."

Rupert nodded. "Yes, people give up on revenge too easily." He got a fiery glint in his eyes. "And maybe we'll shed a lot more of that virgin's blood."

McGoo scowled. "Idiots! She made it quite clear that she's no longer a virgin."

Robin tensed. "Dan, we have to do something. Stella's in danger!"

I hurried toward the Pro Bono Mobile. "You're right, Robin. Let's go make sure she's safe." I tossed a handful of the magic churchkeys to McGoo. "You and Hairy Harry go up and down the street, restore the whole neighborhood. Get rid of these doppelgangers."

Both of them mimed my instructions on how to activate the bottle-opener spell. *"Fsshhht-ahhhhh!"*

I said, "Since the talk show is live, at least we know the perpetrators are still at the studio. We might have enough time."

Because I was better at driving at reckless speed, I took the keys and started the engine with an angry roar. While Robin scrambled to buckle up, I stomped on the accelerator.

We discovered one of Wrex's upgrades to the car.

The old Pro Bono Mobile would have stuttered and coughed before it reluctantly picked up speed. The new engine, however, surprised us. With a buildup of pressure and a roar of steam, the rusty Maverick accelerated like a fighter jet with lit afterburners. The thrust slammed both of us into the backs of our seats.

Somehow, the chassis held together.

I gripped the steering wheel like an overeager strangler and had the presence of mind to honk the horn. Wrex had improved the horn, too, and it blared like a roaring foghorn.

We rocketed toward Stella's eccentric home, hoping to get there before the old-fashioned mob.

CHAPTER 38

We reached the gated and moated community just as full night fell. Donald let us through without even having us put our names on the clipboard.

I hit the brakes and leaned out the window. "Donald! Have you seen an angry mob come through ahead of us? Pitchforks and torches?" The zombie guard could barely hear me over the roar of our car engine.

Now he did check the clipboard, studying the list there. "Nope, not this evening."

Robin shouted, "If a mob does show up, make sure they sign the clipboard." She turned to me. "That'll slow them down."

I thanked Donald and rolled forward. The accelerator pedal was very touchy, and the rockets ignited again, pushing us along. We launched over the moat before the drawbridge had fully lowered into place.

Since it was a residential neighborhood inside a gated community, I watched the speed limit and kept my eyes open for children at play. I hoped they didn't have a noise ordinance.

"I'm more concerned about getting Stella to safety," Robin said, keeping an eye out for an unruly mob in the quiet subdivision. "We might have to use our corporate account and put her into witness protection at the Motel Six Feet Under."

By now, the closing credits must have rolled on *Conversations with Dick the Head*, so we didn't have much time. I pulled the rumbling car up to the librarian's house, which was dark and filled with shadows. One red yard light shone like a danger flare at the head of the drive, casting sharp shadows on the barbed wire fences, the NO TRESPASSING signs, and the lumpy buried lawn-mines.

I shut off the engine, restoring peace and quiet to the neighborhood. As I climbed out of the car, I observed, "Stella looks perfectly capable of defending herself, even against a mob."

"She has a right to privacy," Robin pointed out. "But we need to warn her."

"Maybe I can even pick up the signature sheets, save a trip."

We marched up the sidewalk, and the barbed wire hummed as a breeze picked up. Skeletal branches rattled from dead trees on the property. When we reached the porch, garish security lights blared into our faces, triggered by motion sensors. We froze like a pair of deer staring at an oncoming truck.

I raised a hand, hoping it would be picked up by a security camera. "Hello, Stella! It's Dan Chambeaux and Robin Deyer."

The garish lights did not flicker, but Robin held her leather briefcase like a shield. We climbed the porch, where the welcome mat said *Home Sweet Home*. I rang the doorbell, and tinny Westminster chimes echoed through the house, but we heard no other sounds. No one answered the door.

"You think the Olde Tymers already got here?" Robin whispered, standing at my side. "Some members could have absconded with her while their leaders were on with Dick the Head."

"The Olde Tymers aren't the sharpest criminal minds we've

ever encountered." I rang the doorbell again, but still nobody answered. "It's an awfully quiet mob."

Robin strengthened her resolve. "Legally speaking, Dan, we have reason to fear that Stella Artois is in danger. We should enter the premises and do a wellness check." She tried the knob, surprised to find it unlocked. She glanced back at me. "Ready?"

I reached into my pocket and wrapped my fingers around the .38. "Ready."

Robin pushed open the front door and stepped into the dim foyer. As she peered down the long entry hall, she called out, "Miss Artois?"

No answer. Robin strode ahead, and I followed, looking from side to side, listening carefully.

"I'm surprised she doesn't have active security," Robin said.

Just then she stepped on a plate on the floor.

With a sudden *whoosh*, a stink bomb of greenish smoke squirted around Robin. She waved her hands in front of her face, coughing, then dropped her briefcase. "Can't breathe! What is—"

I dragged her out of the hallway gas cloud, but Robin's eyes fell shut, and her expression went slack. She collapsed in a heap.

Knockout gas.

Or maybe poison gas.

The thick vapor swirled around me, too, but fortunately zombies don't need to breathe, so the gas did not affect me. I dragged Robin by both arms into the reading room where she'd have fresh air.

I hoped she hadn't inhaled too much of the sleeping gas.

I hoped it was only sleeping gas.

The celebrity librarian was overly paranoid—well, maybe

not *overly*—and now her security systems had backfired on the good guys.

I propped Robin in one of the leather reading chairs near the cheery fireplace and set her briefcase next to her. I shook her shoulders and patted her cheeks. "Robin, wake up!"

She didn't stir.

On the table in front of the crackling fire, I saw the lovely little model of Stella's reading room with its model fireplace and foil flames. My attention was drawn to the tiny figurine of Stella in a chair with a book propped in her lap. So carefully painted, every detail, with loving craftsmanship. Even the wrinkles in the fabric of the model's dress were perfect.

The doll was in a different position from what I had seen before.

Then the Stella figurine turned her head and glanced up. Pinhead-sized eyes glowed a bright ruby red. She seemed to be looking right at me, as if I'd interrupted her in a particularly juicy part of the novel she was reading.

I backed away, having reached my quota for creepy stuff.

The house remained silent, and I decided to do more investigating. I shouted in my best Marlon Brando impression, *"Stella!"*

No answer.

After making sure Robin was comfortable, I prowled through the big house in search of the reclusive librarian. Once again, I thought about Linda Bullwer's conspiracy theory. What was Stella Artois really doing?

The cluttered hallways were narrow and threatening, the metal shelves stacked high with books, strange collectibles, odd knickknacks, and more precariously piled books—tons and tons of a hoarder's treasures.

I understood Stella's passion for reading, a librarian

through and through, although a passion for housekeeping might have served her better. I proceeded cautiously, afraid of more boobytraps. Sleeping gas had served to knock out a human intruder, but she might have set equally specific defenses against vampires, werewolves, ghosts—even zombie detectives.

I entered the dining room.

On the long table where Stella had assembled her quaint model houses, a partially completed miniature train set covered the cleared surface. I noted slime tracks on the carpet runner over the hardwood floor, where G. Latinous had made the home delivery of the kit. Stella had already spent hours assembling the model, lining up the tracks, arranging the crossing lights, depot houses, and fake trees.

Then I heard a sound in the big brooding house. It came from behind the two closed sliding doors that blocked off the librarian's mysterious craft room.

The ominous rustling movement came from the other side, and I decided that it was time for me to learn more about arts and crafts.

CHAPTER 39

The double doors rattled and rolled into their sockets when I flung them aside, then I stepped into Stella's artsy-craftsy chamber of horrors.

I drank in the dimness of the craft room, trying to understand what I was seeing. The meek librarian had taken up an unusual hobby since the Big Uneasy.

An architect's light hung over an expansive assembly table, like a full moon over a huge, detailed model of the Unnatural Quarter. Some sections were complete, block by block, house by house, while empty districts were marked with dotted blueprint lines to show what was supposed to be there. Entire streets were laid out, complete with sidewalks, fire hydrants, mailboxes, ornamental trees in perfect geometric order. Houses had black shingle roofs, aluminum siding, perfect lawns, even little toy cars in the driveways.

The model's business district held neat rows of office buildings, restaurants, shops with colorful awnings. The amazing detail extended even to the signs in the windows. Tiny model figures stood on the sidewalks or sat at outdoor café tables. I even saw the distinctive red awning of a Talbot & Knowles Blood Bar.

At the edge of the craft table, a set of fine-tipped paintbrushes soaked in a jar of turpentine, next to little bottles of model paint in a rainbow of colors. Sharp X-Acto knives lay splayed next to a tube of model glue. The air smelled like paint thinner.

One particularly detailed section of the miniature town included Elm Street, complete with the familiar residences around Mary Celeste's townhouse. Stella had even included a little toy bicycle on the sidewalk with a tiny figure of the werewolf furball. Hairy Harry's neighborhood was also there, along with block after block of nostalgic streets that looked freshly installed, new additions to this perfect model of a perfect Unnatural Quarter.

This reproduction was in a whole different league from the exquisite dollhouses Stella had on display elsewhere in the house. But so much of the city was still missing—marked-off gaps of streets, neighborhoods, business districts.

I was suddenly reminded of old Superman comics, where the evil Brainiac shrank Krypton's capital of Kandor and placed the miniaturized city under a dome for his collection.

The craft room had an unsettling hush because the shelves full of books, magazines, newspapers muffled all sounds. Like the rest of Stella's house, the craft room held a ridiculous amount of paraphernalia, collected for its nostalgia value, or maybe just sheer bulk.

"What part of *Keep Out* don't you understand?" demanded a sharp voice.

Stella Artois emerged from the shadows behind the architect lamp. She held a jar of turpentine, sloshing a paintbrush in the murky liquid. "I put out signs saying *No Trespassing* or *Danger*. Some people just cannot be discouraged!"

"I'm easily discouraged," I said. "My partner and I came to check on you, and she accidentally triggered a booby trap. She was overcome by poison gas." I felt angry, even if the defensive system had been an accident. "Is she going to recover?"

"Oh, it's just sleeping gas, nothing to worry about," the librarian said. "I have a right to protect my home from monsters!"

"Robin Deyer was a human lawyer, not a monster, and she was working for you."

Stella scowled. "Humans are easiest to defend against. A little bit of tranquilizer gas—and *poof!*" She set the jar of turpentine down so she could snap her fingers for emphasis.

Then she snapped the fingers on her other hand, which produced an entirely different result.

Moved by an invisible force, the heavy pocket doors rumbled shut and crashed together. I heard the staccato sound of numerous other doors slamming throughout her house.

Stella grimaced. "My magic is certainly powerful, but it's damned hard to control." She picked up one of the tiny paint-brushes and twirled it in the air like an orchestra conductor. "I prefer finesse and detail work ... but, it is what it is."

Seeing the expansive model coming together street by street on her craft table, I had a lot more questions—most important of which was how this meek human librarian had just worked magic to close the doors.

"I will not let you interfere with my greatest craft project, Mr. Shamble!"

I was tense, on guard, but I had not been trained in how to defend myself against a nefarious hobby. "Couldn't you just build a ship in a bottle instead?"

"That wouldn't make up for what I did!" Stella's voice rose to a shout. "I'm trying to atone!"

I'd been sympathetic to the poor woman, sorry about the chaos and attention she had suffered, the paparazzi pestering, the monster love and the Olde Tymers hate. But I never guessed that she might be an evil sorceress herself.

"What are you trying to accomplish with all this?" I gestured to the model of the city. "It's fine work, by the way."

"Thank you." She peered down at the newly installed streets, the buildings, the miniature figures going about their miniature business. I wondered how many other neighborhoods had disappeared just that night ... replaced by doppelgangers. "Even by building a perfect model, I can't bring back the normal world, but I can preserve it! Memorialize the way things should be—step by step, house by house, street by street!"

I turned to the closed doors, wondering if they were magically locked or just shut to impede my rapid exit.

Still explaining, as villains do, Stella grasped the architect lamp and swung the bright light over the tiny Unnatural Quarter. "It's a special spell, Mr. Shamble. Powerful magic that I discovered within myself."

"But you're just a human," I said. "A librarian. You've told the story a thousand times—your papercut, the blood on the *Necronomicon*, the alignment of planets, the phase of the moon."

"To my everlasting dismay, I caused all that horror—and I can never make up for it!" She sulked, and I wondered if the turpentine fumes were getting to her. "But as an unforeseen side effect of the Big Uneasy, I myself received magical powers. You see, on that terrible night thirteen years ago, I was not only shelving the *Necronomicon*—I was doing ... *research*." She whispered the last word. "I was studying spells, hoping I could find some way to improve my life. I had very little respect, no clout, no power—no love life!

"And then I got it all—too much of it. I had to go into hiding. I didn't like the attention."

I turned my gaze back to the huge model. In my experience, evil antagonists were more interested in world domination than in craftsy endeavors. "But what are you doing all *this* for?"

"I can make other people vanish, then replace them with doppelgangers. I made entire unnatural neighborhoods disappear as I practiced my spells." She scuttled over to peer down at two commercial blocks that had recently been added to her big model. "I've gotten so much better at it—five more neighborhoods swapped out just this evening. I'm making a perfect reconstruction of the Unnatural Quarter in its best possible form." She gave a sweet smile, then said, "Before I destroy it all."

That changed my perspective on things.

All the overt explanation made my job as a detective a lot easier. "Is that really a good idea, Stella? Think of the families you'll break up, the monsters you'll harm, the businesses you'll disrupt." A lump formed in my dry throat. "Surely there's something you love about the Quarter, after all these years?"

She indicated her model. "*This* is what I love. I can make it perfect, and then the rest of the world can go back to normal." She pressed a palm to the center of her chest, as if she had a guilty heart. Or indigestion. "I want to make up for the harm I've caused. I want to erase that terrible event."

She scurried into the shadowy piles of boxes, the shelves overburdened with books and knickknacks, and returned with a squeaking library cart that held a huge tome. I recognized its battered spine, its ponderous leather cover, purportedly covered in human skin. The original *Necronomicon*.

Stella opened the book to a certain passage where the words were written in dark red ink. "I have all the resources I need."

"You stole the *Necronomicon* from Howard Phillips? Weren't they already giving you copy number one of the special limited edition?" I paused as a stray thought occurred to me. "Oh, that reminds me to check on the autograph pages—are they finished yet?"

Stella's eyes flared. "This is the only copy that counts—the original volume! Not some cheap facsimile. This is where my blood was spilled. This is what unleashed the magic. *This* is what caused incredible harm to the world."

The tome's spine and corners were now covered with smears of dried mucous, slime stains on the ancient paper and booger globs on the edges. G. Latinous, who specialized in "acquiring things," must have sklurched himself up the drain-pipe to the thirteenth floor and made his way through ducting into the secure publishing offices. He had somehow absconded with the rare volume.

"A librarian should take better care of books," I said.

"Not this one!" Her voice became shrill. "I hired G. Latinous as a consultant, and I told him to obtain the *Necronomicon* for me. He performed his services very well."

"But the pages are gooped. The rare book is damaged."

"I don't care. I'm not a collector."

"Not a collector? I beg to differ." I looked at the heavily laden shelves, the mountains of memorabilia. "If you're in league with the Olde Tymers Society and you want to bring back the good old days, then why did they try to kidnap you?"

She scoffed. "In league with them? They're useless idiots. Rupert and Violet Gleens are pretentious pricks, and I wouldn't join their clubhouse even if they invited me." She crossed her arms over her chest. "No, just like I caused the Big Uneasy all by myself, I have to fix it all by myself."

Trapped there in the sinister craft room, I had to think of the rest of the world, all the unnaturals, not just myself. My friends, clients, and neighbors in the entire Quarter. "Fortunately, I'm good at *un*fixing things."

I reached into my jacket pocket. I could have drawn the .38 and threatened Stella, but I didn't know how a celebrity librarian sorceress would react to a gun.

Instead, I grasped one of the churchkey bottle openers.

"It's Shamble time."

CHAPTER 40

held out the rune-etched bottle opener like a knife fighter wielding a weapon, but Stella didn't even understand the implied threat. "We won't be having any celebratory drinks until I'm finished—and then I'll open champagne, not a beer!"

"This is no ordinary churchkey," I warned. "I can't let you keep those neighborhoods miniaturized and bottled up. I need to set them free."

I hoped the Wannoviches' spell would work on the model as well as the individual doppelgangers. I flicked my wrist and made the appropriate *fsshhht-ahhhhh!* incantation.

When the bottle opener released the magic, translucent ripples flooded over the tiny streets, the miniaturized subdivisions, the nostalgically reproduced tableaus that she had so carefully created.

Stella shrieked. "What are you doing? Noooo!"

"No more doppelgangers," I said. "Unnaturals have worked for thirteen years to get along in this world, to build their own lives, and make a society where we can be just as human as we want to be."

The model buildings began to vanish on the project table—houses, mailboxes, stop signs. The magic wafted through the craft room like mist, and the perfectly preserved constructions popped like soap bubbles and disappeared.

Stella reached out, trying to grab the streets she had reproduced. In her frenzy, she knocked over the jar of turpentine and somehow managed to spill it all over the *Necronomicon.*

Soon the extensive model of the Unnatural Quarter was reduced to just a sketched-out plan on the plywood. As the celebrity librarian wailed, I said, "Look on the bright side— you'll have plenty of reading time in jail."

Stella Artois was not looking for silver linings, though. Her eyes blazed, reminding me of the tiny ruby eyes in the little model of herself in the reading room. But her expression was far more fierce than any doll's.

She raised her hands and unleashed waves of magic. The turpentine-soaked pages in the *Necronomicon* flapped back and forth, although several were clumped together with dried mucous from her slimy accomplice G. Latinous.

As the shockwave hit me, the magic blasted open the craft room doors, splintering the doorjamb. A furious breeze gusted all through her house.

At first, I thought Stella's sorcerous attack was no more than a breaking wind, but then I felt giddy, dizzy. I lost my balance and reached out to grasp the edge of the craft table. I was being … drained. My vision blurred.

I could still hear Stella cackling, shrieking.

When my eyes snapped back into focus, I thought I was standing in front of a funhouse mirror. Dan Chambeaux stood before me in a brown sport jacket decorated with stitched-up bullet holes. I saw my pale skin, strong jaw, handsome features. The fedora was slightly askew to give a rakish private investigator look. The eyes were sharp and clearly intelligent, with the prominent bullet-hole trademark in the middle of my forehead.

A well-preserved zombie … and perfectly duplicated.

I grabbed the .38 from my pocket—and my doppelganger did precisely the same thing, and at the same speed. We faced each other, tense.

I said, "We don't have to fight."

"Yes, we do," he replied.

"I suppose you're right."

He swatted with his hand, trying to knock my pistol away, just as I struck him. Both guns went off at the same time, and the booming reverberation rattled the piled books, newspapers, and magazines. Two bullets ricocheted in opposite directions off the metal shelves.

Stella ducked.

One ricochet struck a pile of newspapers and sent a spurt of paper fragments into the air.

The doppel-Shamble hit my jaw with a hard right hook, a sucker punch. But I'd been expecting it, because I swung my own fist and clipped him on the other cheek. His .38 clattered across the table and dropped off the other side. I was so excited that I fumbled and dropped my own weapon. When it struck the floor, the gun went off, and this time the bullet hit the library cart that held the *Necronomicon*.

"What do you expect to accomplish?" I demanded of my double. "You can't become me. Sheyenne, Alvina, and Robin will know the difference."

"I have all your memories and your mannerisms. Once I get rid of you, I can take over. I'll be the most powerful zombie P.I. in the Unnatural Quarter, and then I can help Stella Artois recreate everything that you just ruined."

"I ruined it on purpose." I admit, it's difficult to make a snappy comeback to yourself.

I threw myself on the doppel-Shamble, punching and wrestling. When the two of us crashed onto the craft table, our body weight was too much for the rickety legs to bear. The architect lamp wavered like a searchlight chasing a mosquito. The plywood surface cracked and tumbled, spilling paint-brushes and turpentine, tubes of model glue and bottles of paint.

I tore myself away and scrambled across the floor on my hands and knees. I had dropped the magic churchkey when Stella unleashed her magic attack, but now I grabbed it, aimed at my doppelganger. I made the vehement gesture as if wrenching the cap off a very large bottle of beer. *"Fsshhht-ahhhhh!"*

My doppelganger staggered back, then straightened and laughed before he came at me again. I twisted the churchkey again and again. To no effect.

"You can't un-self-duplicate," he said.

He threw himself on me and knocked the churchkey loose. He pummeled me with his fists, but I gave as good as I got. We were evenly matched (and apparently I was a pretty good fighter). It was like shadowboxing.

We circled and circled. I looked for a way out. I could run, but the doppel-Shamble would be just as fast. We fought ourselves to a standstill, glared at each other. And I didn't like me when I was angry.

Stella grabbed the *Necronomicon* from the cart, squeezing it as if she could wring more magic from its pages.

Doppel-Shamble punched me. I reeled backward, then hit him in the stomach. He raised his fists, ready to lunge again.

Suddenly, Robin loomed up behind him in the doorway, staring at the scenario. She held one of Stella's dollhouses in her hands. Without hesitation, she smashed it down on the duplicate's fedora-covered skull. He reeled, and she clubbed him again with the model house, breaking it into countless pieces.

My doppelganger collapsed, unconscious.

I stared at her, rumpled, bruised, and out of breath. "Thanks, Robin."

She snatched the dropped churchkey from the floor and extended it. "Maybe you can't un-self-duplicate, Dan—but let me give it a try."

She made the gesture and the sound, activating the spell.

The doppel-Shamble groaned and lifted his chin just in time to swirl, ripple, and fade away.

"How did you know which one was the real me?" I asked, still breathing hard. "We were identical."

She gave me a secretive smile. "Dan, I've worked with you for so many years, I just *know*."

Then Stella Artois made her move.

CHAPTER 41

ometimes, the cases fight back, with a vengeance.

S I didn't have time to feel like a whole man again, or at least a whole zombie, before the crisis doubled. I really longed for the days when Stella was nothing more than a shy, lonely librarian. Not only had she forgotten her calling to revere literature, she apparently had no qualms about damaging books.

Stella grabbed the heavy, snot-stained tome from the library cart and scuttled out of her craft room of horrors. I had never seen a librarian move so fast. "You leave me no choice! I have to erase the Big Uneasy!" she shouted as she bolted through her dining room. "I'll destroy the *Necronomicon.*"

I understood the threat. If she destroyed the original *Necronomicon,* surely the magic that had caused the Big Uneasy would unravel.

Robin brushed off my rumpled jacket. "We've got to stop her, Dan!"

While fleeing, Stella bumped into the dining room table, jostling the model houses and dislodging the miniature train set. The massive tome clearly weighed her down.

"I bet she wishes she had the paperback version," I said to Robin as we headed after her.

The librarian ran for the reading room and its roaring fireplace, and I realized exactly what she meant to do. "Stella, stop! You don't know what you're doing."

She glared at me over her shoulder. "Yes, I do—I've researched the subject."

Trying to increase her lead, Stella yanked the overloaded bookshelves in the hall. With a resounding crash, the metal units toppled in an avalanche of books, including several sets of the Shamble & Die mysteries. The mountain of reading material formed a roadblock that slowed us down.

I climbed over the barricade of collectible literature, while Robin scrambled over boxes, pushing them aside to make a clear path. A full set of "signs of the zodiac" limited-edition display plates shattered on the floor.

Stella kept running, obviously full of regrets, but fiercely determined. "I'll do what I have to do!" She held up the powerful tome as if threatening a hostage.

Robin drew back her arm and hurled her leather briefcase, and it struck the celebrity librarian right on the chin, knocking her backward. Stella dropped the *Necronomicon* on the floor with a thud.

While she scrambled to retrieve the thick book, I tripped over boxes of rare, numbered comic-book action figures, but I couldn't worry about cultural damage until after we had prevented Stella from unwinding the Big Uneasy.

The librarian got moving again, knocking down more shelves as she retreated to the reading room and its hungry fireplace.

We bounded after her, and Robin grabbed her briefcase along the way. "We've got her cornered now!"

Filled with power, though, Stella was exactly where she wanted to be. She faced us next to the overstuffed chairs, holding the turpentine-soaked *Necronomicon* in front of the fireplace. With a wild expression, she yelled, "It's the only way! I remember the good old days. I just want peace and quiet." With her other hand, she picked up a cast-iron poker. "I want a normal world, where monsters are *fictional*."

She brandished the poker in the air, held the heavy volume in her other hand. Turpentine had covered the ancient pages, but maybe the dried mucous would have a fire-retardant effect. Or, blob snot could be especially flammable. Either way, I didn't want to risk it.

I lurched toward her, hands outstretched, while Robin closed in from the other side.

Seeing that she had no escape, Stella threw the rare, original *Necronomicon* into the fire.

I gasped, and Robin cried out. The flames immediately caught on the dried human skin of the cover, igniting the turpentine-soaked paper. The magical book popped open, and pages flapped in the rising blaze, turning brown, then black.

Stella collapsed into the nearest reading chair. "There, it's done! The Big Uneasy is over."

I reached for the fireplace, but the book was fully engulfed in flames, the paper falling into gray ash. The spine bubbled and crackled, and the leather turned black. Bitter smoke filled the room.

Robin stared in disbelief and horror. I held up my hands, expecting to disappear at any moment, just like my defeated doppelganger. The whole Unnatural Quarter, which I had just restored with the magical churchkey, would suddenly become as empty as Mary Celeste's Elm Street.

I wondered if Mary herself would lose her unexpected spare set of arms, or if she would vanish entirely along with the rest of the unnaturals.

Without the Big Uneasy, the ghosts would disappear, along

with vampires, werewolves, harpies, and litches. Albert at the Ghoul's Diner would be gone. Alvina might return to a normal little girl ... or she could just die.

Everything in the world would change.

And I would be a dead detective, instead of a zombie detective.

Stella huddled in her reading chair, sobbing and laughing, as if she couldn't decide on the proper emotions.

Eventually, the turpentine, paper, leather, and blob snot burned out, and the flames died down. The original *Necronomicon* was just a lump of ashes now, glowing orange in the coals.

With grim resignation, I looked at Robin in a fond farewell. I felt great love and appreciation for my firebrand lawyer partner. I wished Sheyenne could be here with me. She would be gone, too....

"Robin ... I have so much to say—"

She waited, and I waited.

Stella peered into the fireplace, her mouth open in surprise. She used the poker to jab the pile of glowing coals, stirring up sparks.

"How long is this supposed to take?" I asked.

Robin brightened. "Maybe it's not going to work!"

Stella rose from the reading chair. Her hair was loose and sweaty, the wire-rimmed glasses askew on her face. "No! The Big Uneasy has to change. The *Necronomicon* is destroyed."

A tiny voice shouted out nearby. "You are such a disappointment!"

Inside the Plexiglas display case, the perfect miniature figure of Stella rose up from her facsimile reading chair. The demonic ruby eyes glared up at the horrified librarian, ignoring me and Robin. "I'm done with being a tiny afterthought!"

Stella pressed her hands against her face in horror. "No!"

The tiny model's eyes shimmered and glowed. The air between her and the real Stella rippled with fumes, as if someone had sprayed too much air freshener. Stella cringed like the Wicked Witch of the West doused with water, while the tiny doppelganger in the display case glowed.

She vanished, as did Stella.

After a heartbeat, the figures exchanged, with the real librarian now duplicated and locked inside the case, while a double of Stella Artois—a better, more normal version—appeared standing next to us in front of the fireplace. She nodded with satisfaction and picked up the display case. "I hate complainers," the doppel-librarian said in a voice dripping with disapproval.

Without so much as a glance at us, the doppel-Stella tossed the case into the flames, where it smashed. Stella's tiny model voice squeaked and shrieked, but the model burned into embers in a matter of seconds, adding to the ash pile from the original *Necronomicon*.

The Stella duplicate wiped her palms on her dress, which was identical to what the real Stella had worn. She eyed me up and down. "Are you all right?"

"Wrinkled and bruised maybe, but I'll live," I said. "Or whatever."

"Good." The duplicate Stella straightened her glasses and rearranged her mussed hair. "People need to move on and pay attention to the good *new* days instead of longing for things that used to be." She looked at me and Robin. "I trust we'll keep these details between us?"

"Works for me," I said.

Robin considered. "I agree wholeheartedly. I think I prefer this version of Stella Artois." She rubbed a finger along her chin. "In fact, now that we've had thirteen years to get used to it, I prefer this version of the world, too. I'm glad to work with Dan. I've come to consider the unnaturals to be friends as well as clients."

With the matter settled, as if nothing untoward had happened, the new Stella went to a side table and picked up a large stack of papers—the signature sheets I had previously delivered.

"Meanwhile, I made a commitment that I intend to honor. I have a lot of work to do." She found a pen. "I'll deliver these to Howard Phillips Publishing by tomorrow."

CHAPTER 42

We gave a slightly modified story to the UQ Police Department, conveniently leaving out the part about the evil librarian doppelganger swap. We blamed the theft of the valuable *Necronomicon* on the blob consultant, which was in fact true.

Robin held her yellow legal pad, and the ensorcelled pencil was poised to take notes. She nudged the writing implement to signal that she didn't want these private words recorded.

I said, "The doppelganger Stella Artois shouldn't have to pay for the crimes of her original."

"There are other guilty parties." Sheyenne sniffed. "We know all the trouble caused by Rupert and Violet Gleens and their Olde Tymers flunkies. They can take the fall, if need be."

The mob riled up by their old-fashioned leaders had marched off to lynch the celebrity librarian, but when gathered together their current membership was only seven people. After the inciting episode of *Conversations with Dick the Head*, the angry crew had first made a vengeful charge—embarrassingly—to an incorrect gated community, and by the time they got Stella's correct address, Donald had closed the gate from his guard shack.

When the zombie guard asked each of the rioters to write their names down on his clipboard, five of them wandered away, not wanting to identify themselves. That left only Rupert and Violet Gleens, who were stymied by the shark-and-croc-odile moat (especially in their constrictive old-fashioned clothes). They, too, had eventually dispersed, vowing to be offended another day.

"Maybe everyone doesn't need all the answers," Robin said. "In law school I had an entire semester on the importance of being vague."

Sheyenne began to do the wrap-up paperwork. She was glad I had survived and that the Big Uneasy had remained uneasy, but disappointed that the entire adventure had produced few billable clients. "What are we going to tell Linda Bullwer when she decides to write about this in her next novel?"

I remembered her suggestions after she'd been attacked by the pit bull dogwood. "She's a ghostwriter. She'll make up something interesting, I'm sure."

"I'm glad the Unnatural Quarter is back to normal," Alvina said. She was especially glad to have McGoo back.

The kid had already made several Monstagram and Sick-Tok posts after taking selfies with her two half-daddies. Since the vampire girl didn't show on the images, the photo just looked like McGoo and I were standing awkwardly far apart with nobody between us.

Sheyenne glanced toward our kitchen and let out a wistful sigh. "If only I could get rid of that malicious mold as easily as those doppelgangers vanished."

"I'm teaching it to play tic-tac-toe," Alvina interjected. "To keep it occupied."

McGoo strolled into the offices, his freckled face flushed. He slurped his cinnamon latte and sighed with delight, a sound that reminded me of the bottle-opening spell. He reached into his pocket and dropped a handful of leftover churchkeys on

Sheyenne's desk. "Never been used. Thought you'd want to keep them as souvenirs, now that the case is all wrapped up."

"Still a lot of loose ends," I said.

"I can wrap up the loose end of the slimy accomplice," he said. "We put out an all-points bulletin and captured G. Latinous before he could flee the Quarter. The snot was starting to run! He was a slippery sort."

I remembered how the big blob had rolled over the would-be Olde Tymers kidnappers at the library. "How did you get him under control?"

McGoo snorted. "Sprayed a couple of gallons of decongestant on him. He won't cause us any more headaches, sinus or otherwise."

"I'll be glad to focus on my normal cases," Robin said. "I have a court date with a cyclops."

"Hey Shamble," McGoo said with a grin. "How many zombies does it take to shingle a roof?"

I was reluctant to answer, but the dreaded joke was reassuring. In a way. "I don't know, McGoo. How many?"

"Depends on how thinly you slice them!" He guffawed, and Alvina appropriately giggled.

"I'm glad to have the real you back, McGoo."

I HEADED FOR HOWARD PHILLIPS PUBLISHING. ALVINA TAGGED along with me, but I didn't mind, since I appreciated the time with my vampire half-daughter. She was getting to be a real partner. For her own part, Alvina was happy with the prospect of getting more free books.

When the elevator opened on the thirteenth floor, Mavis and Alma Wannovich greeted us in the reception area. The big sow waddled up to Alvina for her expected hug, and Mavis was also happy to see me. "Thank you for all your help, Mr. Shamble. Stella Artois already delivered the signature sheets, and our special edition is back on schedule. She has a remarkably neat autograph. A thousand signatures, all identical—I think that librarian must be superhuman!"

The witch didn't realize how close to the mark her comment was.

The Wannoviches led us through the publishing cubicles to their editorial offices. Howard and Philip Phillips were waiting for us there, smiling with pride. "Mr. Chambeaux! Let us express our gratitude for your protective and investigative services."

Howard added, "Yes, please send us your bill as soon as the paperwork is done. We have everything we need from you at the moment."

Philip needed the last word. "But please keep providing inspiration to Linda Bullwer for her next Shamble & Die adventure, though at present she's hard at work on her *Necronomicon* sequel. We hope to announce it along with the publication of our special collector's edition."

"I want my own copy of the *Necronomicon*," Alvina said.

"You're not old enough," I said. "And it's very expensive."

Mavis cackled. "We can get you a complimentary copy!"

"One thing still bothers me.... Actually a lot of things bother me, but there's one relevant detail here." I looked around the busy offices. "If the original *Necronomicon* was so powerful, why didn't the Big Uneasy unravel as soon as the book was burned? I watched it go up in smoke. Now, I don't understand the legal and magical loopholes of spells, but it seems to me that once the original copy was destroyed, all this

—" I spread my hands. "Shouldn't the unnaturals have disappeared?"

Standing at the office door, Howard and Philip shared a guilty glance. "Actually …" Howard began.

Philip broke in, "Ahhh, the copy we kept on display wasn't really the *original* original."

I frowned. Even Mavis looked surprised.

Howard started to explain. "You see, the display case held a prototype, copy number zero of our facsimile reproduction."

"Accurate down to the last detail!" Philip said. "The original copy is one of a kind. We wouldn't risk exposing it to the grubby hands of the …" He shuddered. "General public!"

"Can't trust people," Howard said. "Not these days."

I remembered the security systems, the guards, the hype about the battered copy on the pedestal. "So, it was just a fake that burned to ashes?"

"The word 'fake' sounds so … pedantic," Philip said.

"It was a truly accurate, high-quality reproduction using only the finest materials," Howard said. "A stellar example of the quality of books we produce."

I didn't know whether to be relieved or angry, and chose instead just to be confused.

"The original original is locked in Howard's desk drawer in our executive offices," Philip said. "Where it's perfectly safe."

The twin publishers stood shoulder-to-shoulder, nodding in unison.

A ruckus from the receptionist's desk cut off further conversation. I heard raised voices, a growl, then a howl. "I demand to see my editor—right now. Make my day!"

"That sounds like Hairy Harry," Alvina said.

"Dear me, we did have an appointment to discuss his manuscript," said Mavis, hurrying toward the front.

The Phillips brothers stayed behind with a dismissive comment. "We don't deal directly with authors."

In the lobby, the rogue werewolf cop confronted the gargoyle receptionist, who remained stony-faced. "I'm sorry, sir, but we can't accept unsolicited arguments."

Hairy pounded a paw on the countertop, then turned to glare at us as we came around the corner.

Mavis said, "There's no need for shouting, Mr. Harry. We generally reserve our shouting for editorial meetings."

"I want to know the status of my book!" he snarled. "You have the only copy of the expanded manuscript. It needs to be published before word gets out. There's another whole chapter to add, thanks to Shamble here." His furry brows drew together. "In fact, I'm going to engage the services of his lawyer partner. I'm going to sue. I don't like being duplicated!"

"Nobody does." I thought of the brawl with my own doppelganger.

He whirled. "What did you say to me, punk?"

Mavis Wannovich continued trying to calm the rogue cop. "Alma and I were discussing your book in detail, sir. It's not quite ready for publication yet, I'm afraid. It needs some editing to make a few of the scenes more realistic."

Alma snorted, trying to communicate something. Mavis looked down at her sow sister, then nodded. "Yes, in particular chapter eight."

Hairy Harry bristled, but Alvina bounced in. "Right now, all editorial discussions are premature."

I recognized language she must have learned from the legal homework Robin had given her.

"We haven't even reached terms on the book deal. I already have my social-media marketing plan, but first you'll have to make an acceptable offer." The kid smiled, showing her pointed fangs. "Remember, I'm his agent, and you should deal with me."

W E ALL MET FOR LUNCH AT THE GHOUL'S DINER. ALVINA WAS hungry for a snack of Unlucky Charms, and Robin said she could always use a good peanut-butter-and-jelly sandwich. I decided I could tolerate Albert's gray-goop daily special.

I wanted to relax after the recent mayhem, but Robin considered it a working lunch and brought her notes on the cyclops double-vision lawsuit. As we slipped into our favorite booth, I was glad to see Mary wearing a waitress apron. She bustled from customer to customer, refilling water glasses. When she saw me sit down, she snagged the volcanic pot of oily coffee and poured me a cup without asking.

"I see you've been promoted," I said.

"Hostile takeover," Mary replied. "Albert is slow to make decisions, so Esther and I are both waiting on tables."

The harpy flounced among other customers, snapping and snarling at them until they agreed that their food was acceptable after all.

"We're both making a lot of tips." As she talked, Mary reached out with her extra set of hands, laying down napkins and silverware in front of Robin and Alvina.

On the other side of the diner, Esther dropped a plate with a crash, spilling smoky globules of something like chili into the lap of a frightened mummy.

Robin's brow furrowed. "I'm surprised Esther's getting tips, when they can see how much better your service is."

Mary snickered. "They tip her to make sure she *doesn't* wait on them, so that way I get all the customers." She raised her multiple arms. "I can handle it, but I might not be working at the diner for much longer." She leaned closer and dropped her voice to a whisper. "Yesterday, a modeling representative came in—and I have a job coming up! Hand modeling for a new fingerprint pad company. I'm going to be a star!"

"In my book, you already are," I said.

She took our orders and hurried off, handing the ticket to Albert, who slaved away over his hot cauldrons and noisome refuse bins.

As I glanced at all the unnatural customers, I smiled to myself, reassured to see the fully restored neighborhoods of the Quarter. Nothing was normal, but it was a new normal.

And this city is just the way I liked it.

ACK! KNOWLEDGMENTS

I want to give a special zombie hand to all those who helped my undead detective shamble on. Rebecca Moesta for her constant inspiration, tolerance, and editing skills. MiblArt in Lviv, Ukraine, who did the beautiful redesign of the entire Dan Shamble series even with their country at war and while they were ducking in and out of bomb shelters., and our proofing team of Aysha Rehm, Zach Ritz, Holly Smith, Nikki Winchester, and Patricia Weber for lending their eyeballs to spot insidious typos.

And to the special Kickstarter backers who helped this project come alive: John and Ana Klanjac, Scooby Doom (!!!), James Johnston, Josee Dubois, Erwin Hans Busch, and Andrew Bulthaupt.

ABOUT THE AUTHOR

 **Kevin J. Anderson** has published more than 170 books, 58 of which have been national or inter-national bestsellers. He has written numerous novels in the Star Wars, X-Files, and Dune universes, as well as unique steampunk fantasy novels *Clockwork Angels* and *Clockwork Lives*, written with legendary rock drummer Neil Peart. His original works include the Saga of Seven Suns series, the Wake the Dragon and Terra Incognita fantasy trilogies, the Saga of Shadows trilogy, and his humorous horror series featuring Dan Shamble, Zombie P.I. He has edited numerous anthologies, written comics and games, and the lyrics to two rock CDs. Anderson is the director of the graduate program in Publishing at Western Colorado University. Anderson and his wife Rebecca Moesta are the publishers of WordFire Press. His most recent novels are *Gods and Dragons*, *Dune: The Heir of Caladan* (with Brian Herbert), *Stake*, *Kill Zone* (with Doug Beason), and *Spine of the Dragon*.

Read All the Cases of
Dan Shamble, Zombie P.I.

Death Warmed Over

Unnatural Acts

Hair Raising

Working Stiff

Slimy Underbelly

Tastes Like Chicken

Services Rendered

Double-Booked

To Order Autographed Print Copies

of this book and many other titles
by Kevin J. Anderson
please check out our selection at

wordfireshop.com